Christmas Presence

Four Festive Stories

Liz Hedgecock

WHITE RHINO BOOKS

Copyright © Liz Hedgecock, 2017, 2021

All rights reserved. Apart from any use permitted under UK copyright law, no part of this publication may be reproduced, stored in a retrieval system, or transmitted, in any form or by any means, electronic, mechanical, photocopying, recording or otherwise, without the prior written permission of the copyright owner.

This is a work of fiction. Names, characters, businesses, places, events and incidents are either the products of the author's imagination or used in a fictitious manner. Any resemblance to actual persons, living or dead, or actual events is purely coincidental.

ISBN-13: 979-8753505996

Contents

Christmas Eve At The Bookshop	1
The Most Wonderful Time Of The Year	22
A Christmas To Remember	45
The Case Of The Christmas Pudding	59
About The Author	97

Christmas Eve At The Bookshop

'I'm afraid it really is closing time.' Jemma gently took a Gladys Mitchell novel away from one of the Golden Age crime fans, then steered the two women upstairs, through the ground floor of Burns Books, and towards the front door.

'When will you be reopening?' one asked. 'I know you're only just closing, and it's Christmas Day tomorrow, but—'

'On the twenty-eighth of December,' Jemma replied. 'I'm sure you'll have lots of books in your Christmas stockings. Enough to keep even you busy.' She knew for a fact that both the Golden Age crime ladies had visited the bookshop alone the previous week to buy each other a present, and she felt sure they would swap the books once they had read them.

'One hopes so,' said the other Golden Age crime lady, 'but one can never be sure what the family will buy one.' She brightened. 'Perhaps there will be book tokens.'

'Perhaps there will,' said Jemma. 'Anyway, Merry Christmas!' She beamed at them and opened the door.

'Merry Christmas,' they chorused, and walked into the bright lights of a festive Charing Cross Road.

Jemma shut the door, locked it, and turned the sign round to *Closed*. Then she leaned on the door, closed her eyes, and exhaled. *Finally, time for Christmas.*

'Have they gone?' Raphael asked, in a stage whisper, and Jemma jumped. She hadn't heard her boss come upstairs, but he could be remarkably stealthy when the mood was upon him. He advanced into the room, resplendent in a navy suit, tartan waistcoat, pink dress shirt, and orange bow tie.

'I certainly hope so,' said Jemma. 'I was starting to wonder if some of our customers would still be here on Christmas morning.' She smiled as she imagined them waking from their slumbers in armchairs and against bookshelves, rubbing their eyes and yawning. 'Perhaps we could organise a bookshop sleepover—'

'Not this year,' said Raphael, with a visible shudder. 'This year, our job is to exchange presents, lock up both the shops, and enjoy Christmas.'

'Meow,' said Folio, who had followed Raphael upstairs and was swishing his ginger tail in a let's-get-on-with-it manner.

Jemma gazed around her. The ground floor of the shop was in fairly good order, since their Christmas celebration with the customers had happened downstairs. The parquet floor gleamed with polish, as did the mahogany counter, and lights twinkled through the shop window. However, some of the customers had still managed to bring coffee cups, glasses, streamers and the occasional party hat upstairs, and dumped them on any available surface. 'Aren't we going to tidy the shop first?'

Raphael surveyed the scene. 'Do we need to?'

Jemma nodded. 'It makes sense to do it now, while the rest of the team are still here. If we all muck in, we can get it done in ten minutes. To put it another way, do you want to come in early and clean on the first day back?'

'When you put it like that…' Raphael sighed. 'I suppose that's why you manage both bookshops.'

Jemma grinned at him. 'And that's why you let me. I'll tidy here and bring crocks down if you'll go downstairs and let the rest of the team know. I'm sure they won't mind.' She scooped up a tangle of paper streamers and carried them to the bin.

***

A few minutes later, the shop looked much more orderly. Jemma stepped back to admire her handiwork. Her life had changed so much in a few short months. In her previous job she had lived to work, whereas now— Well, she still hadn't got her work-life balance exactly right, but working in a magical bookshop – no, *two* magical bookshops – was certainly much more fun. And they had secured the future of the shops, hopefully for a long time to come.

'Jemma!' called Carl, from downstairs. 'Are you nearly finished?'

Jemma gave a guilty start. 'Almost,' she replied. She surveyed the ground floor of the shop again. As they were closed for Christmas, it seemed silly to have a pile of presents under the tree and Christmas stockings put up. She tidied those away, then took herself to non-fiction and pulled out books for a New Year display: planners, diaries, self-help books, diet and exercise manuals... *I'll do the same at my own shop*, she thought, putting the books on the counter. *But perhaps not tonight*. Tonight, she and Carl were having a quiet night in with a takeaway and a bottle of wine. Tomorrow they were spending Christmas with Carl's family, and they would visit her parents on Boxing Day. Jemma suspected Carl and her father would bond over Lego, while her mother would nag Carl about his next play, which he hadn't begun writing yet.

'Jemma!' called Carl. 'Presents!'

'All right, I'm coming!' Jemma shouted. She collected as many rogue coffee cups and glasses as she could manage, and went downstairs.

As predicted, it had taken the team very little time

to get things straight on the main floor of the bookshop, and now they were relaxing. Raphael and Giulia, the owner of Rolando's delicatessen along the street, sat holding hands in adjacent armchairs. Maddy, Jemma's assistant at the Friendly Bookshop down the road, was squished into an armchair with Luke, Raphael's assistant, who was sporting a black party hat with red streamers. Em, the shop's new barista, was leaning on the café counter, while Carl, her predecessor, was sprawled across an armchair, long limbs everywhere. Folio and Luna sat side by side on top of a bookshelf, tails curled round their paws, like a pair of mismatched bookends: one ginger, one glossy black. But the stone floor had been swept, the glasses cleared away, and the dishwasher behind the café counter had just enough room left in it for Jemma's crockery. The huge space, the former crypt of a lost medieval cathedral, looked spick and span, if a little depleted. Several people had come in that day to do last-minute Christmas shopping, and distinct gaps showed on the bookshelves.

'We can restock the shelves when we reopen,' said Luke firmly. 'It'll probably be quiet then, anyway.'

'I suppose,' said Jemma, secretly glad not to have to do any more work.

'In that case,' said Em, 'do you mind if I go? I've swapped presents with everyone except you, and I said I'd try to be at my parents' for nine.'

'Sure.' Jemma retrieved Em's present from her special hidey-hole under the counter. She had put off buying it until the last minute, first uncertain what to buy, then unsure whether to trust her former best friend, given the odd shop-related happenings she had been involved in. However, the events of the last few days had shown her that she had no cause for suspicion, and she had bought Em a little amethyst pendant, her birthstone, which she hoped she would like.

Em beamed at her, reached into her shoulder bag, and presented a book-shaped parcel. 'Bet you can't guess what this is – but you'll have to wait till tomorrow.'

'I know!'

They hugged each other, and Em waved to the others as she left. 'Don't go on partying without me too long,' she said. 'If I come back to work and find you all hungover…'

'Be off with you,' said Raphael. 'I don't get hangovers.'

That's a point, thought Jemma. *Now I'm an Assistant Keeper, and I don't ever get coughs or colds any more, I wonder if I'd still get hangovers? What a brilliant perk!* She saw Raphael regarding her with an amused expression, and attempted to look businesslike.

'Right,' said Raphael, rubbing his hands, 'presents!

This is our reward for being so organised and diligent. As well as three days' holiday, of course.'

'Of course,' said Luke. 'Hang on a minute.' He ran upstairs, coming back with his arms full of parcels wrapped in black paper and tied with red ribbon. He presented the one on top, which was suspiciously rectangular, to Jemma. 'Merry Christmas!'

'Thank you!' Jemma retrieved Luke's wrapped gift from under the counter. She had put a lot of thought into it. After all, there were plenty of things to avoid with regard to Luke, particularly as he was cutting out meat and animal products whenever possible. In the end, she had bought a cookbook called *Vegan Vampire: High-Protein Recipes for an Energetic Life*. She handed the gift to Luke.

'Should I open it?' he asked, with a sly grin.

'Yes, go on,' said Jemma. 'I'm dying to open mine.' She undid the red bow and the neat wrapping, which she suspected Maddy had helped him with. 'Oh,' she said, gazing at the book in her hand.

'Don't you like it?' asked Luke, crestfallen. 'I thought you'd enjoy trying something new.'

'Yes,' said Jemma, 'it's lovely. It's just that the only classic vehicle I've ever had anything to do with is Gertrude.'

'I'll have you know that Gertrude is a state-of-the-art, up-to-the-minute camper van,' said Raphael.

'Classic vehicles?' said Luke. 'I bought you a book

of Transylvanian recipes. You're always talking about broadening your culinary horizons.'

He sounded so certain that Jemma checked the cover of the book. 'Could it be someone else's present?' she asked. 'The tag had my name on, but…'

Luke shook his head. 'I don't think I've ever bought a book on classic cars. But maybe you're right, and your book is one of these other ones.' He grinned. 'I guess we'll find out soon.' He put his pile of gifts on the counter. 'Let's see what I've got.' He opened Jemma's gift, which was wrapped in shiny red paper with a black ribbon, and no less neatly packaged, since Maddy had helped. 'Oh, um…' His expression was a mixture of distaste and fascination.

Jemma craned over to look at the book. '*Hunting, Shooting and Fishing*? I definitely didn't get you that. Or buy it for anyone else.' She frowned. 'Could I possibly have wrapped the wrong book? It's been busy lately.'

'You definitely didn't,' said Maddy. 'I helped both of you wrap those books. You couldn't possibly have got it wrong.' She wrinkled her nose. 'There's something fishy about this.'

Jemma tapped *Hunting, Shooting and Fishing*. 'You could be right.' She surveyed the room. 'This bookshop has a habit of producing the books we need at the right time, but we don't need books on classic cars or hunting.' She considered the presents she had bought. 'Let's peek inside the present I got for Folio. Maybe it's just a mix-up with books.' She had bought Folio a large tin of his favourite salmon, and a deep-gold velvet collar which matched his eyes. She retrieved his present, which she had wrapped in fish-patterned paper and put a fish-shaped tag on to distinguish it from Luna's. She glanced at Raphael. 'Do you want to open it, or shall I?'

'Go on, I'll look,' said Raphael. He opened one side of the present carefully, peeped in, then snorted. 'I'm guessing you didn't buy Folio a tin of peaches, Jemma.'

'No, I did not!' said Jemma. 'Is there anything else?'

'Yes, there is,' said Raphael. He tipped the parcel carefully, inserted two fingers, and extracted one of the thin silver chains which they used for securing aggressive or misbehaving books, complete with a padlock. He offered it to Folio, who turned away with his nose in the air.

'Something's definitely up,' said Maddy. 'I wonder if it's only Burns Books, or if it's the same at the Friendly Bookshop?'

'There's one way to find out,' said Jemma. 'Maddy, shall we go and see? I've got your present over there, so hopefully it won't be affected if it is just this shop.'

'Likewise,' said Maddy, looking worried.

'In that case, I might put the kettle on,' said Carl. His brow furrowed. 'Is that wise, in the circumstances?'

'Absolutely,' said Raphael. 'If our supply of tea is affected, things are in a very bad way indeed. Off you two go, and we'll have a cup waiting when you return.'

***

'Do *you* think it's both shops?' asked Maddy, as they walked the short distance to the Friendly Bookshop.

'Who knows?' said Jemma as she strode along. 'I don't understand why it's happening at all. I mean, in the last week we've beaten a dangerous and powerful adversary, saved Burns Books from being demolished, sold loads of books, and had no customer complaints.' She pulled out her keys. 'Well, here goes nothing.'

She unlocked the door, trying not to hold her breath, flung it open, then switched on the lights. 'See, all fine.' The shop was just as they had left it a couple of hours ago: somewhat understocked, and with the Christmas stockings and wrapped presents removed from the displays, but clean and tidy.

Maddy went to the left-hand drawer of the counter and pulled out a beautifully wrapped parcel – book-shaped, of course – which she handed to Jemma. 'Merry Christmas.' She gave Jemma a shy smile. 'I hope you like it.'

'I'm sure I shall,' said Jemma. She and Maddy had worked together in the Friendly Bookshop for a while now, so if Maddy didn't know her taste in books... She opened the right-hand drawer of the counter and produced a parcel rather less neatly wrapped than Maddy's. Maddy was a fan of all things Gothic, as was Luke, and Jemma had managed to track down a beautiful hardback edition of Ann Radcliffe's *Gaston de Blondeville* with gilt-edged pages and a black ribbon page marker, courtesy of one of her book suppliers, the mysterious Elinor Dashwood. 'Go on, open it.'

'Are you sure?' said Maddy, glancing at Jemma and biting her lip.

'Of course.' Jemma fought the urge to cross her fingers.

Maddy slipped her finger under one of the flaps, then pulled the wrapping paper away. 'Erm...'

'Don't tell me you've already got it,' said Jemma. 'I was sure you didn't have this one.'

'Well, I don't have a dog,' said Maddy.

Jemma glanced at Maddy's book: *Tricks Your Dog Can Do*. 'That is *not* what I got you,' she said. 'Should I open mine?'

Maddy shrugged. 'Why not join in the fun.'

Jemma opened her present, feeling guilty for disturbing the beautiful bow and the meticulous pleats, and held up a copy of *Teach Yourself*

Synchronised Swimming. 'No?'

'No,' said Maddy, glaring at it.

'So something's wrong with both bookshops,' said Jemma. 'I wonder what it is.'

'Who knows,' said Maddy with a sigh, slipping *Tricks Your Dog Can Do* into her tote bag. 'Let's go back to Burns Books, have a cup of tea, and see if we can work it out.'

***

Jemma was silent as she locked up the Friendly Bookshop and walked to Burns Books with Maddy. Her brain was in a whirl. *Why are the bookshops doing this? Is it the bookshops?*

A thought slunk into her mind. Before Em had left, could *she* have swapped the presents? It was possible, though given how busy the bookshop had been, her chances of doing anything but serving hungry and thirsty customers were minimal at best. But why would she do that? And more importantly, how could Em have entered the Friendly Bookshop unseen by either Maddy or herself, found their presents, switched the books, and rewrapped them to look identical? Jemma's initial disappointment was replaced by a tidal wave of guilt that she had doubted her friend yet again, with no real grounds to suspect her. Then guilt gave way to anger, and she marched towards Burns Books determined to sort things out once and for all.

She pushed the door of Burns Books so hard that the bell almost fell off, jangling on its spring like an alarm.

'What is it?' asked Maddy, following her in and closing the door rather more gently. 'Have you thought of something?'

'Not as such,' muttered Jemma. 'But I know one thing, that's for sure.'

Maddy grimaced, then locked the door and followed her downstairs.

'Anything to report?' asked Raphael. They were sitting around a café table nursing mugs of tea, with a large teapot in the middle. Two empty seats, and two empty mugs, waited.

'It's just as messed up over there,' said Jemma, flopping into one of the chairs and pouring tea for herself and Maddy. 'And no, I haven't a clue why. Any ideas here?'

One by one, everyone shook their heads. Jemma fixed Raphael with a gimlet eye. 'Has the shop ever done this before?'

Raphael took a sip of his tea and considered. 'The shop can be a little . . . mischievous. But no, nothing quite like this. Then again, we've never exchanged presents; I've never had so many staff. So there's nothing to go on.'

'Maybe the shop doesn't approve of Christmas,' said Jemma, setting her mug on the table with a sharp clack. 'In that case, we should just clear this away. If the shop's spoiling things, there isn't much point in trying to celebrate.' She went to a pillar, untied the tinsel wrapped around it, and pulled it down. Then she addressed the ceiling. 'Is that what you want?'

Predictably, there was no response.

'Fine.' She moved to the next pillar. 'If you're going to mess things up, maybe next year we won't bother at all,' she muttered as she undid the sparkling tinsel.

'Jemma…' murmured Raphael.

'What?' Jemma dropped the tinsel at her feet and walked to the next pillar. 'Come on, you lot, let's get this over with. If the shop's sulking, it can do it on its own while we enjoy Christmas somewhere else.' She reached for the next piece of tinsel, and stumbled as the floor lurched. 'What the—'

'Oh no,' murmured Maddy. 'Not again.'

The lights flickered, and with a buzz, one of the chandeliers went out.

'Maybe you should stop doing that, Jemma,' said Raphael, very calmly.

A book whizzed from the bookshelves and whacked Jemma on the elbow, then fell to the floor. She retrieved it and turned it over: *A Christmas Carol*. Folio yowled. The cats were both standing, backs arched and hackles raised.

'I'll go and hold the stockroom door closed,' said

Raphael, rising swiftly. 'If you can contain things here, please do.' He staggered on his way to the great oak door as the floor undulated beneath his feet.

'What do we do?' asked Luke, looking around helplessly.

'I don't know!' cried Jemma. 'Maybe put up the tinsel?' She reached down and grabbed a piece. 'Ow!' It was burning hot. The air was hot, too: warm, sticky, and clinging, as if they had suddenly been transported to a tropical island. A desert island. And while everyone else was still in the bookshop, suddenly she felt very alone.

Jemma blinked. The room went out of focus, then came back about two feet to the left. But it was still decorated, with pretty green and yellow dots just like Christmas-tree baubles twinkling at the edge of her vision. In fact, they seemed to be closing in on her...

Something thudded to the floor beside her, and she jumped. *Did another book hit me? I didn't feel anything.* She looked down, and saw *Teach Yourself Synchronised Swimming*. *I must have brought it from the other shop*, she thought, bending to retrieve it. When she straightened up, the room lurched like a ship on a stormy sea. 'Whoa!' she cried, stumbling downhill and crashing into the shop counter. Grateful for something stable to lean on, she rested her head on it and let the book drop.

And everything paused.

'What the…' murmured Carl, from the café area.

The floor was still at a slight angle, but the rumbling had stopped and the air seemed a little less clammy.

Cautiously, Jemma raised her head as a bead of sweat trickled down her back. Carl was spreadeagled against the café counter as though he had been glued to it, holding closed as many cupboards and drawers as he possibly could. Maddy and Luke were protecting the fantasy and Gothic literature sections, which happened to be next to each other, and also holding hands. Giulia, meanwhile, was glaring at the cookery section, daring, just daring anything to disobey her. As far as Jemma knew, Giulia possessed no magical abilities, but she was prepared to bet that those books would behave themselves.

'What do you want us to do?' she whispered. 'What did I do?'

'What *did* you do?' asked Raphael from the doorway. He walked to the counter and inspected *Teach Yourself Synchronised Swimming* without picking it up. 'Ahhh.'

'Well, go on,' said Luke. 'Tell us.'

'I could be wrong,' said Raphael, 'but I think the shop is jealous.'

'Jealous?' said Maddy. 'Of what?'

'Us,' said Raphael. 'We've all brought presents for each other, including the cats.' Folio and Luna looked at each other, then at him, and swished their tails. 'But we haven't got anything for the shop,' he whispered.

'Oh,' said Jemma. 'Well, I can sacrifice *Teach Yourself Synchronised Swimming,* if that helps.'

'We may not need to,' said Raphael. He went to a nearby armchair, fetched the silver book chain and padlock which had replaced Folio's present, and hung it around the Christmas tree. As he did so, the shop seemed to level itself. The off-kilter feeling Jemma had had, like water in one ear after swimming, disappeared.

'Ohhh,' said Carl. He ducked behind the counter for a moment, then reappeared holding his socks. He opened one of the cupboards, put a wrapped candy cane in each sock, and laid them on the café counter.

They blinked as the chandelier above them lit up.

'Hold on,' said Jemma. She ran upstairs, tumbled the self-help and good-intentions books she had gathered into a box, and carried it to the stockroom. In exchange, she selected a book box at random and took it downstairs with her.

Raphael raised an eyebrow. 'Under the tree?'

'Yes, under the tree,' she said.

Luke removed his party hat and perched it on one corner of the cash register at a rakish angle.

Maddy undid her black lace hair ribbon and shook out her long dark hair, then tied the ribbon in a neat bow on the highest branch of the Christmas tree that she could reach. She stepped back to admire it. 'Look!'

Their eyes followed her pointing finger. Where the book chain had hung was a gold velvet collar with a fish-shaped brass tag dangling from it, on which was engraved *Folio*.

'Open the box of books, Jemma,' said Raphael. 'Let's see what we have.'

Holding her breath, Jemma fetched a pair of scissors and snipped at the tape, uncertain whether to expect Christmas books, magic books, or another genre altogether. When she opened the cardboard flaps, she found the box full of mystery novels. 'Oh!' She looked at the crime shelves, which were full of gaps, ransacked by the Golden Age crime ladies and many others that day.

Maddy came over and peered into the box. 'The shop wants us to fill the shelves.'

'I think you're right,' said Jemma. And when they began, the new books fitted the gaps exactly. 'This shouldn't take long,' she said, grinning. 'Could you go and get some more?' Maddy, Carl, and Raphael hurried towards the great oak door, and as Jemma watched them go, smiling, she realised that the bookshop, now cosy rather than tropical, smelt of cinnamon, plum pudding, and mulled wine.

Once the shelves of the shop were groaning with

books again, everyone exchanged presents, with more confidence than they would have shown an hour before. Maddy went to the counter, picked up the book sitting there, and handed it to Jemma. Somehow, *Teach Yourself Synchronised Swimming* had transformed into the latest Marian Keyes novel. 'I'm glad everything is back to normal,' she said. 'Or as normal as it ever gets. May I look?' She gestured at her tote bag.

'Of course,' said Jemma, crossing her fingers.

Maddy unslung the bag, peeped inside, then whooped with joy and gave Jemma a huge hug. 'Wherever did you find it?'

Jemma grinned. 'Oh, you know, in a bookshop.' She turned to Luna, who was curled in a complicated cat yin/yang arrangement with Folio. 'Come along, Luna, time for us to go home. Raphael's looking after you tomorrow, so you can play with Folio again.' Luna rose, stretched, and opened her mouth in an enormous yawn.

Raphael smiled. 'Merry Christmas, everyone.' And he kissed Giulia beneath a sprig of mistletoe which Jemma could have sworn wasn't there before.

※※※

'Good presents?' asked Carl the next morning, as they sat amid a sea of wrapping paper in their pyjamas, in Jemma's flat above the Friendly Bookshop.

'Oh yes,' said Jemma, laughing. 'Even if Maddy

and Giulia both got me the latest Marian Keyes book. But this is lovely.' She touched the silver necklace with a pretty J in script, which Carl had put on for her.

'Thank you for mine,' said Carl, running his hand over the burgundy linen notebook embossed with his initials. It was refillable, and she hoped he would write many plays in it. 'What did Raphael get you?'

'He gave me this.' Jemma opened a square black box to reveal a thin silver bracelet. Two beads were strung on opposite sides: one deep yellow, one purple. 'It's very pretty, but I'm nervous about wearing it in case it does something.' She closed the box. 'I hope he likes his bow tie. Assuming it is a bow tie again, and not a pasta bow or a dead fish.'

'Mraoww!' Luna jumped on the bed, resplendent in her new green velvet collar, her eyes all pupil in the winter sunlight.

'I suppose that means we should get dressed and be on our way,' said Jemma. But she stayed where she was, a pensive expression on her face.

'What's up?' asked Carl.

Jemma rummaged among the presents on the bed and showed him a copy of *The 4-Hour Work Week*. 'Em gave me this, but I can't tell if it's her real present or if it's stayed swapped. Remember, we exchanged presents before the shop had sorted itself out.' She grinned. 'Maybe it's another Marian Keyes book in disguise.'

Carl took the book, glanced at it, then tossed it onto the bed. 'Never mind work,' he said. 'It's Christmas now. You'll have to wait and see.'

He leaned over, and as he kissed her, Jemma smiled to herself. *I suppose I shall,* she thought. *After all, who knows what surprises the new year will bring?*

***

If you're new to the world of the Magical Bookshop, you may have some questions! Find out how Jemma came to the bookshop, the tricks the shop has played in the past, and what's special about Gertrude the camper van in the Magical Bookshop cozy mystery series. The first book in the series is *Every Trick In The Book*: http://mybook.to/bookshop1

The Most Wonderful Time Of The Year

'You do realise the place will be heaving,' said Simon, throwing a pair of rolled-up socks into the suitcase.

'That's all part of the atmosphere,' said Pippa. 'London at Christmas! The lights and the shops—'

'Ah yes, the shops.' Simon sat on the bed. 'Can we try not to max out the credit cards?'

'There'll be pre-Christmas bargains—'

'Which you'll hide in the wardrobe and forget about, Pippa Parker, and then end up re-panic-buying at the last minute.'

'Freddie will love it.' Pippa placed her jeans in the case with an air of finality.

'Mmm.' Simon looked around the clothes-strewn room. 'I just wish we didn't have to bring the kitchen sink.'

'Well, that's babies for you.' Pippa ran through her

mental checklist. Ruby's Moses basket, changing mat, pushchair, sling, nappies, wipes, three times as many clothes as she ought to need... She still wasn't sure how they would carry everything onto the train. How did they manage when they lived in London? Pippa had a sudden vision of the doors closing, shutting them and their equipment inside while Ruby wailed on the platform. She shook her head to dissolve it. 'It'll be fun!'

***

'I feel sick, Mummy,' said Freddie, as the train rocked through the Home Counties. 'Are we nearly there yet?'

Pippa brushed Freddie's hair out of his eyes. His forehead was warm. 'Maybe in half an hour.'

'Can I have sweets?'

'Not if you're feeling sick.'

Freddie's mouth turned down even further, and he wrapped his arms round his tummy. Pippa sighed, and settled in her seat. Her left arm ached from supporting Ruby, who sprawled across her like a little starfish, fast asleep and breathing heavily. 'You'll be fine once you're off the train.'

'I won't.' His gaze wandered across the table to Pippa's phone. 'Can I play a game?'

'Who knew phones cured travel sickness,' Simon remarked softly, as they watched Freddie zap aliens with his thumbs.

'Amazing.' Pippa looked at Ruby. 'She's being so good.'

Ruby smiled in her sleep. Seconds later Pippa retched as the smell assaulted her nostrils. 'Urrh! How can she do that and stay asleep?'

'The smiling assassin.' Simon shifted as far away as he could. 'I wish she wouldn't look so pleased with herself.'

'She won't when I change her nappy.' Pippa gazed out of the window at the fields speeding by, and consoled herself with thoughts of Christmas shopping.

***

'Let's go and enjoy London!' Pippa's enthusiasm was as brittle as a glass bauble. Between getting everyone and everything off the train, finding the right Tube line, and listening to Freddie moan while she and Simon managed the luggage and Ruby between them, she wondered if a Christmas shopping trip with the children might be her worst idea ever.

The chilly winter air was a smack in the face after the tropical hotel foyer. 'Is there food in London?' Freddie quavered.

'Freddie.' Pippa manoeuvred Ruby's pushchair round a gaggle of students carrying backpacks. 'We lived in London until we moved to Much Gadding. Did you starve?'

Freddie shook his head miserably. 'That was

different.'

'The Christmas lights are on!' Pippa exclaimed. High above the street, an army of Santas delivered presents from their sleighs, making a brave show in the grey sky.

'Is that it?' whined Freddie.

'It'll be better when it gets dark,' Pippa assured him.

'What about lunch?'

'We'll find lunch,' soothed Simon. 'Good idea, Fred-Fred. I know somewhere nearby.'

'Yeah!' Freddie grabbed his hand and swung it, grinning, and Pippa reflected on the time she had spent planning the trip. *Oh well.* She frowned at a strange sound drifting down the street.

'Is someone torturing a duck?' Simon said, laughing. Freddie looked up at him with big, worried eyes.

'Don't be silly,' said Pippa, firmly. 'Let's go and find out.'

The source of the noise became apparent a few steps further. A small crowd made it invisible, but the cause was obvious. 'Bagpipes!' cried Pippa. She wheeled Ruby towards the crowd. 'Come on, Simon. I don't think Freddie's seen a bagpiper before.'

'I doubt he'll see one now,' said Simon, peering at the crowd.

As luck would have it, a couple of people peeled

away as they approached. The piper was in full rig: kilt, sporran, jacket and Balmoral cap.

Simon nudged Pippa. 'Bet he's a bit chilly,' he said, nodding at the piper's kilt.

'Oh, honestly,' said Pippa. She studied the piper as he puffed, his face impassive under his hat. He was young, and from what she could see, rather attractive. Surely there were easier ways to make a living? Then she noted the instrument case in front of him, lined with notes and coins. *Fair enough.* She glanced back at the piper, and he was looking right at her. Was that the ghost of a smile? She studied the window of the department store. 'Oh! I wanted to come here!'

'Such a coincidence,' remarked Simon. 'What's the draw?'

'The most expensive watch in the world,' said Pippa. 'It's on display here. I read about it on the web.'

'What's so special about it?'

'Well,' said Pippa. 'It has a false front completely encrusted in diamonds and rubies, to look like a Christmas present. And when you lift the cover, the watch plays a Christmas carol. It has a memory of twenty-five songs, so you never know which it will be. And it's accurate to a fraction of a second every thousand years. You can't even buy it yet, and they're only making ten of them.'

'Wow,' said Simon. 'It sounds horrible.'

'Doesn't it?' said Pippa. 'I can't wait to see it.'

Simon laughed. 'All right. We'll go and see the watch, then lunch. Deal?'

Pippa beamed. 'Deal.'

***

'Why don't you just ask?' Simon indicated a shop assistant hovering on an invisible line and clearly itching to come over.

Pippa wriggled. 'I can't remember what it's called. I can't exactly ask where they keep the horrible watch, can I?'

Simon smirked. 'I bet people do. Excuse me!' he called. 'Where would we find the, um, *Christmas* watch?'

The assistant beamed from ear to ear. 'The Santa Special Festive Forever Timepiece?'

'That sounds about right.'

'It's on the third floor, in Accessories, Jewellery and Watches, Statement Watches, Seasonal, Limited Edition.' Her smile was well-practised and slightly strained. 'Just get the lift to the third floor, then follow everyone else.'

'There you go,' said Simon. 'Let's get this over with. I kind of want to see it myself now.'

Ping! Third floor for accessories, jewellery and haberdashery!

But as the lift doors opened and they unpacked themselves, the store tannoy crackled into life:

'This is a special announcement for all shoppers. Due to an incident, we have had to close the doors of the store. Please do not be alarmed. This is a safety precaution and anyone wishing to leave the store may do so at the main entrance, after a bag and body search. We hope things will return to normal shortly and will keep you updated. Please continue to browse and to shop. Thank you.' The woman making the announcement sounded incredibly embarrassed.

'Someone's stolen something!' Pippa muttered, under her breath.

'What did the funny lady say?' asked Freddie.

'Don't worry, Freddie, it's nothing. We're, um, just going down here.' Pippa steered the pushchair right, which seemed to be the direction most people were heading in.

The saleswoman had been correct. As they walked along the Parkers joined more and more people converging on Accessories, Jewellery and Watches, Statement Watches, Seasonal, Limited Edition, until a large crowd stood round a glass case, ducking, diving and standing on tiptoe to catch a glimpse of the white plinth and the empty space on top.

***

'Well, that was exciting,' said Simon. 'Shall we get some lunch?'

'Yeah!' cried Freddie. 'Are there baked beans in London?'

'I imagine so,' said Pippa. She felt odd: deflated, almost. She wasn't *that* bothered about seeing the watch, but for it to disappear... Who had taken it, and how? The display case seemed completely undamaged.

A plump woman in a royal-blue coat tapped the glass. 'It was here, in the case! I *saw* it! And the next time I looked, it had gone!' She blinked hard and fumbled for a handkerchief. A leather-jacketed man tried to push past her, and she elbowed him viciously in the ribs.

Pippa stepped away from the people jostling to reach the case and scanned the area for an assistant. A young man in store uniform cowered behind the nearest counter, where a throng of people were firing questions at him. He actually had his hands up.

The crackle of a short-wave radio approached, and a grizzle-haired man wearing a sharp grey suit came with it. 'Approaching the area, over.' He holstered the radio smoothly and clapped his hands. 'All right, folks! Happy for you to see the show, but please be considerate of our staff. The police will arrive shortly.'

The throng around the counter drifted towards the empty case. 'We only wondered what was going on,' said a woman with an artistically draped scarf, in cut-glass tones.

'Of course, madam,' soothed Sharp Suit. 'If I

could tell you, I would.'

'When did it happen?' asked Pippa.

Sharp Suit regarded her for several seconds before answering, as if sizing up how much of the truth she could handle. 'The absence of the Santa Special watch was discovered a few minutes ago. We immediately secured the exits, then sent someone to the tannoy. Now if you'll excuse me—' He moved a pair of handbags from a raised platform and mounted it. 'Everyone! You are welcome to come and look, but do give other people room. And watch your bags and purses.'

People were flooding from other parts of the store, fighting their way genteelly to the glass case, taking full advantage of spike heels, elbows, and umbrellas.

'Mummeeee,' Freddie whimpered, pulling her sleeve. 'Don't like it.'

'We'll go in a second, Freddie.' Pippa found her phone and took a picture of the empty glass case, its white satin cushion still indented with the impression of the watch. There was a lock on the side of the case, she noted, but only a standard one.

Three more assistants approached bearing armfuls of red rope and metal stands, which they set up to form a passageway.

'Right!' called Sharp Suit. 'To make sure everybody gets a chance to see, you can have two minutes at the case, then we'll ask you to move on.

When Gareth pings his bell—' He nodded to the assistant at the counter, who smacked the bell with some relish. 'That is your signal to go.'

Everyone who wasn't already holding their phone rummaged in bags and pockets, then turned their backs on the case and held their phones at arm's-length.

'What are they doing, Mummy?' Freddie asked, wide-eyed.

'They're taking selfies, Freddie. Photos of themselves with the empty case.'

'Why, Mummy?'

Pippa considered how to explain social media to a three year old. 'I think they're trying to catch the moment.'

'Why, Mummy?'

'Let's go for lunch.'

Several people stared as Pippa and her family left the Accessories, Jewellery and Watches, Statement Watches, Seasonal, Limited Edition department of their own free will. Gareth's bell pinged, and an *Ohhhhhh* of disappointment rose from the vicinity of the glass case.

Three more assistants hurried by: one with an armful of selfie sticks, one with camping stools, and one wheeling a hostess trolley piled with soft-drink cans. Simon grinned. 'The Three Kings.'

'Excuse me!' called a young woman standing in

31

the queue. She was checking her hair in the screen of her phone. 'Is it – is it as good as Twitter says?'

'It's remarkable,' said Pippa.

The woman's mouth dropped open. She nodded thanks and adjusted her hair with renewed determination.

***

After a cursory pat down and a frisk with a hand scanner – 'They're hoovering me, Mummy!' giggled Freddie – they were permitted to leave the store. Pippa pushed the heavy glass door and the strains of 'Scotland the Brave' filled the air.

'Still going,' observed Simon, taking control of Ruby's pushchair and steering it away from the long thick snake of people waiting to enter the store.

'Looks like it.' Pippa glanced over and smiled at the piper, but he showed no sign of recognition. She studied him more closely. *Hmmm.* While almost identical in feature, this piper had a mole on his left cheek. 'Hang on a minute.' The drone seemed to be reaching a climax. She found a pound coin, and once the noise ceased, threw it into the case.

'Thank you,' said the piper, and his chiselled face showed the beginnings of a smile.

Pippa stepped forward. 'Excuse me for asking… Are you a different piper from the one half an hour ago?'

His very blue eyes crinkled. 'That would have been

my brother Calum.' He had a soft Scottish accent. Indeed, he sounded like the people in the remote village where her parents now lived.

'You're Highlanders?'

'That's right.' He nodded at the case and Pippa saw a small heap of business cards. She took one and read:

Ross Bros
Pipers at Large
Entertainment for Any Occasion

'I take it you know what's happened in the shop,' she said.

'I've heard something, yes. The shop kindly let us use their facilities to change over between shifts.' He looked away as Pippa raised her eyebrows. 'We only have one outfit between the five of us,' he explained. His face was perhaps a shade redder than before.

'So how long have you been piping outside here?'

'Today, or in general?' His eyes twinkled.

Pippa grinned. 'Both.' Out of the corner of her eye she saw Simon tapping his watch

He finally cracked a smile. 'Today, maybe half an hour. I was late starting because of the . . . commotion. As for in general, we've been here three days. The store hired us for the week as part of their Christmas campaign.'

'Oh!' Pippa exclaimed. It was the piper's turn to raise his eyebrows. 'I thought you were buskers!'

'We are. The store saw a video of us and invited us down. Apparently we're a good draw for the tourists. They follow the sound of the pipes and stay to shop. Shame we couldn't all come, though.'

'How many of you are there?' Pippa tried to imagine what their family parties must be like.

'Including cousins, eleven pipers.' He grinned. 'But the car only holds five.' He put the blowpipe back in his mouth, which Pippa took as a signal that the conversation was over.

***

'I just don't get it.'

Simon gestured with a plastic spoon. 'What? How so much food can be aimed at a baby's mouth and yet end up everywhere but?' Ruby crowed, and an orange lump plopped onto the tray of her high chair.

Pippa sighed. 'I just accept that as a fact of life.' Freddie harpooned half a fish finger and stuffed it into his mouth. 'I meant the watch thing.'

'Does it matter?' Simon poured some more beer. 'We're on holiday, and the shop will be insured. Don't waste your time worrying.'

'I know those things.' Pippa chewed her lasagne. It possessed a ready-mealish quality she found strangely comforting. 'But I don't understand how they did it. I mean, people have been staring at that watch the whole time. It was locked in a glass case, which is intact. And then it's gone. It isn't as if someone could just walk up, unlock the case and get the watch out while it was unattended. It's never unattended!'

Simon levelled off a spoonful of baby food and aeroplaned it towards Ruby. 'Maybe a master hypnotist came, put everyone in a trance, got the keys, got the watch, then clicked his fingers as he left the area. Everyone comes round, and the watch is gone.'

'Oh, give over.'

'All right.' He scraped the spoon round the jar. 'The thief actually stole the watch in the night and replaced it with a copy made of a super-fine secret substance. Someone somewhere presses a button, and the watch disintegrates into a fine dust invisible to the naked eye.'

'I preferred the first one.' Pippa gulped down a large forkful of lasagne. 'Here, I'll take over with Ruby. Your food's getting cold.'

'Thanks.' Simon handed Pippa the loaded spoon and sawed at his steak. 'Wow. I think they gave me a rubber one.'

'Euww.' Pippa opened her mouth wide at Ruby, who copied her, and slid the spoon home. 'Yes! Two more to go, and then pudding.' She wiped Ruby's face. 'It isn't even a locked-room mystery. It's a locked-*case* mystery. With an audience. It's impossible!'

'Well, you know what that Sherlock Holmes chap says,' said Simon.

'Enlighten me.'

'I might be paraphrasing.'

'That's fine.'

'Eliminate the impossible and what remains, however improbable, must be the truth.'

'Mmm.' Pippa made a face at Ruby, who laughed, and got another spoonful put away. 'I wonder if there was a psychological moment.'

'A whuh?'

'*You* know. Something that distracted everyone just for a second or two.'

'It must have been longer. No one could get to the case, unlock it, take the watch, and relock the case in that time. Not without someone noticing.'

Pippa put the last spoonful of food into Ruby, and slowly screwed the lid onto the empty jar. 'You know what? You're absolutely right.'

'Elementary, my dear Holmes.'

'Watson.'

'No, *you're* Holmes, remember. I'm Watson, who makes the daft remark to get you on the right track.' Simon smiled, and then fed the smile with steak and chips.

'Perhaps you are.' Pippa found the packet of rusks and gave one to Ruby, who clamped it in her gums, dribbling with pleasure. 'Perhaps you are.'

***

'Really, Mum? That *is* interesting. Give my love to Dad, won't you? Yes, we will come up for New Year. Yes, I'll remember the marmalade. Bye, Mum. Bye.'

Pippa clicked *End Call,* and thought. She opened her browser and typed in *Ross*, plus the phone number from the business card. The result made her cackle.

'Is it getting any clearer?' asked Simon.

'Might be,' said Pippa. 'I need to see one more thing.'

'How long will it take?' Simon said, raising his hand for the bill.

'Once we're in the store, five minutes.'

Simon rolled his eyes. 'Come on, then.'

As they walked back to the store, Freddie wailing '*Again*, Mummy?', Pippa spied the piper, now playing 'Loch Lomond'. On impulse, she went over and whispered in his ear. The noise which followed was not part of 'Loch Lomond', nor of any other recognisably Scottish tune. The blowpipe fell from his mouth and he stared at her, aghast.

'It's OK,' said Pippa, putting a hand on his arm. 'I get it.'

***

As Pippa had expected, the third floor was still crowded. A string quartet played 'Diamonds Are Forever', deckchairs were set in rows, and a small concession stand sold snacks, drinks, and souvenirs of

London. All in all, it seemed quite a good day out.

Ping! went Gareth's bell, and another set of viewers filed obediently past, discussing what various minor celebrities had said about the event on social media. A couple of them had stuck around to sign autographs; a small table stacked with notebooks stood close by. A film crew and a news reporter were also working the crowd.

Pippa looked for Sharp Suit. Ah, there he was, sauntering down from Ladies' Handbags, chatting to a fluttery female assistant. Pippa stepped into their path. 'Excuse me?'

Sharp Suit paused, hands in pockets. 'How can I help?'

'I think I know what's happened to the Santa Special.'

His eyebrows rose, slowly. Then he grinned. 'I've heard many theories today. I don't suppose one more will hurt. Go on, hit me.' He removed his hands from his pockets and made a show of bracing himself.

Pippa walked forward, cupped her hand to his ear, and whispered for a minute.

After one sentence, she felt him stiffen.

After half a minute, he was trembling.

By the time she had finished his shoulders sagged, and sweat shone on his forehead.

Pippa stepped back, and like a doomed automaton, Sharp Suit turned towards her, his face a mixture of awe and horror. 'All right,' he croaked. 'You've been very clever. Tell them, then. Tell them all.' He lifted his hand, sighed, and let it fall.

Pippa put a finger to her lips and regarded him speculatively. 'What's it worth,' she said, 'for me *not* to tell them?'

In an instant Sharp Suit looked as if all his Christmases had come at once. 'Madam,' he purred, 'if you would come this way? I think we have exactly what you require.'

***

'I could get used to this.'

Pippa and Simon sat side by side on club chairs in the toy department, watching the children play. An assistant was helping Freddie manoeuvre rather a fancy remote-controlled car. Ruby, meanwhile, had a big box of soft bricks, and her own assistant to stack them before she swept them down, giggling.

Simon cased the joint. Everyone was busy, with enough noise for cover. He nudged Pippa. 'Come on, tell me.'

'I did say I wouldn't tell anyone.' Pippa smiled faintly.

'I'm not anyone!' Simon protested.

Pippa grinned. 'OK.' To be fair, she'd been *bursting* to. She lowered her voice to a murmur. 'Here's how it went. You were right about the psychological moment. That was the cleverest bit of the whole thing. Something guaranteed to distract everyone and make them look away from the watch.'

Simon thought for some moments. 'No, I'm not going to get it.'

Pippa smiled like a cat with a dish of cream. 'It was the tannoy announcement itself. When we were getting out of the lift everyone looked the same way, to see where the sound was coming from. Even Ruby. You can't help yourself, even if it's only for a moment. And a moment was long enough for our first operative to make the watch disappear.'

'So someone did take the watch?'

'Yes. It wasn't him, though.'

Simon rubbed his forehead. 'I don't think I've ever felt more Watsonish. Just tell the story.'

'All right. So the plinth that the watch sits on is hollow inside. When the tannoy starts, Operative 1 presses his remote control. The cushion the watch is resting on drops on one side, like a trapdoor, then resets. The watch falls to the bottom of the case – a soft landing, I presume – and Operative 2 gets to work.'

'Operative 2?'

'Yes. He's on the floor below, dressed as a maintenance man, fiddling with one of the ceiling tiles.'

'So that's why you went to the second floor before we came up here!'

'Exactly. Remember the ladder and the man-at-work sign propped against the wall?'

'Nope.'

'Neither did anyone else. Operative 2 reaches into the ceiling space, pockets the watch, puts the ceiling tile back, and leaves. He probably removes his overalls in the nearest bathroom. No one cares what he's doing anyway, they're heading for the third floor.'

'But wouldn't he be frisked on the way out?'

'Nope. He looks completely different when he leaves. Plus he's well known to the staff.'

'I'm completely lost. Not Suit Man, then?'

'No, he's strolling upstairs to do crowd management. Operative 2 leaves dressed as a bagpiper. The Ross brothers change outfits in the staff toilets; they've been doing it for three days. No one would think anything of it. Except that the watch is now in the piper's sporran. It still is, in fact.'

'So the bagpipers are some sort of Scottish jewel-thief gang?' Simon's voice had the slow, reasonable quality of someone struggling to take it all in. 'And Suit Man was in on it?'

'Better than that.' Pippa grinned. 'That's why I rang Mum; I figured a large collection of fit young Highland bagpipers would be pretty conspicuous. Turns out they're quite well known there. A couple of the Ross brothers were a bit wild growing up and had some brushes with the law, but they were too clever to get caught. Just. After a very near miss, they set up as security consultants.'

'Poachers turned gamekeepers.' Simon laughed. 'Brilliant.'

'Exactly. When I checked the phone number from the pipers' card on the internet, it took me to the piping business *and* the security firm.'

'So they were hired to steal the watch.' Simon frowned. 'But why?'

'Haven't you seen the crowds in the store?' Pippa pulled out her phone and opened Twitter. 'See? Number one trending topic: #watchrobbery. Associated hashtags: #whereswatchy, #OxfordStWatch, #SantaSpecial. This photo of the empty case has been retweeted half a million times. How much would it cost to buy that sort of publicity? And they might set up someone finding it to create another buzz. I might suggest it to Sharp Suit – I mean Kevin.'

'Ah yes, Kevin.' Simon snorted. 'You gave him the fright of his life.'

'He'll get over it. And I'm sure handing me two thousand pounds in store vouchers made him feel a whole lot better.' Pippa opened her purse and fanned them out. 'Very satisfying.'

'I take it you are planning to spend those.'

'No, I thought I'd frame them.' She paused. 'Don't be daft, of course I'm going to spend them! Let's start with these toys, then order a hamper for Mum and Dad – with marmalade, obviously – and maybe a handbag for me, earrings for Sheila, something from accessories for Lila and Suze . . . and what would you like?'

Simon grinned. 'An unbroken night's sleep. But I'd settle for cufflinks. Or posh socks.'

Pippa's eyes narrowed. 'Are we getting old?'

Simon got up. 'Back in a minute.' He returned with a bottle of champagne and a box of chocolates. 'For when the kids are asleep.'

Pippa stood up and kissed him. 'I like your style.'

'Good.' Simon embraced her, a little awkwardly given his burdens. 'Now let's get a trolley and spend those bad boys. We have work to do.'

'Freddie! Time to go!' Pippa called. Freddie's lower lip began to wobble. 'No, you can take one with you.' Pippa pointed to the stack of toy cars. 'Choose your favourite colour.'

'Really?' Freddie's face lit up.

'Really. And we'll take a box of blocks, too.' Pippa fetched one and showed it to Ruby, who thumped her fists on it in approval.

'This could get messy,' said Simon. 'I just hope the train can take it.'

***

Later, much later, they left the store, loaded with bags and boxes. Lights twinkled in the street.

'Let's get a taxi to the hotel, drop the presents off, and see the lights.' Simon kissed the top of her head.

'That's an excellent plan.' Pippa lifted her face to Simon's, and 'Auld Lang Syne' drifted towards them.

'A week before Christmas?' said Simon. 'I think he's peaked too soon.'

'Oh, I wouldn't say that.' Pippa indicated the pile of money in the instrument case. 'They'll do just fine.' She winked at the piper, then realised it was a different one again. But he grinned and winked back, and the song modulated into a new tune.

'What's that one?' asked Simon.

'"The Bonnie Lass o'Fyvie",' Pippa replied. She couldn't stop herself smiling.

'Is it, indeed.' Simon shifted the bags to his other hand and took her arm.

'It is.' Pippa looked back, and the piper, foot tapping, nodded to her. She might be wrong, but she had a distinct feeling that she hadn't seen the last of the Ross Bros, Pipers at Large.

***

If you've enjoyed this Pippa Parker short mystery, why not try the cozy mystery series, set in and around the quaint English village of Much Gadding. The first book, in which Pippa arrives in Much Gadding, is *Murder at the Playgroup*: http://mybook.to/playgroup

A Christmas To Remember

'What will you do today, Randolph?' asked Estella, cutting her breakfast slice of pineapple into pieces with a fruit knife, then pouring us more tea. 'I take it you have no Civil Service business to attend to this weekend.'

I gazed through the door to the veranda into the garden, which was quiet. Deepak and Prabir would come out and tend it later, when the temperature had risen. While I found Calcutta in December pleasantly cool in comparison with the summer months, the servants thought otherwise. Then again, it was fresh enough to require a jacket. 'I could go for another ride, I suppose, unless there is anything you wish to do? After all, it is Saturday.'

Estella's gaze slipped past me, and presently Avik, our head servant, approached. 'Your post, madam,' he said, proffering several envelopes and a small parcel.

'Nothing for me?' I asked.

Avik regarded me gravely. 'I am afraid not.'

'Never mind,' I said, with a smile. 'No post means no emergencies, crises, or catastrophes, and that has to be a good thing. Especially so close to Christmas.'

'It's a shame we won't be home for Christmas this year,' Estella said, looking up from a letter. 'I know the children are disappointed; letters aren't the same at all. But work…'

'Ah, work,' I said, with a sigh. Being a senior employee in the Indian Civil Service carried its own responsibilities, and as for Estella's work – well, that was as predictable as the Indian weather. 'Perhaps next year.'

'Yes,' she said. She opened her last letter, scanned it and replaced it in its envelope, then reached for the package, giving me a quick, appraising glance.

The hairs on the back of my neck prickled. I tried not to stare as Estella examined the package, turned it over to read the return address, and placed it unopened beside her breakfast plate. 'My plans have changed somewhat,' she remarked. 'I am wanted at Government House.'

'On a Saturday? Isn't that rather irregular?'

She smiled. 'No more irregular than anything else.' She stood, and picked up the parcel. 'It is not a great matter; I should return by noon. I shall go and change, as when I dressed this morning I was not expecting to meet with the viceroy.'

'No, dear,' I said, trying not to stare at the parcel. For inside, I felt sure, was my Christmas present; Estella's furtive look had told me so. 'Will you require the carriage?'

'Yes, I shall,' said Estella, and with a nod, she left the dining room.

As soon as her footsteps had receded, I sprang up and opened the dining-room door. Estella was vanishing into our bedroom, just as one would expect. But knowing Estella, there was more to it.

In all the years of our marriage, I had never once been able to get at or guess my Christmas present before the day. I had examined stray bills and receipts, questioned the servants, and even followed Estella on occasion, but to no avail. This year, though, I had the advantage, since she had to leave the house on business and that parcel, while comparatively small, was too bulky to be carried in a handbag.

My musings were disturbed by Sujit entering the dining room via the veranda. 'I'm so sorry, sahib,' he said, bowing to me. 'I thought you had left.'

'Not quite,' I said, sitting down and sipping from my almost empty cup of tea.

'Shall I wait?'

'No, that will not be necessary.'

'You are nearly finished, sahib. Should I stand outside?'

'What a good idea.' I waited till Sujit had retreated,

then rose from my seat and tiptoed through the other door. I could hear Estella moving about in the bedroom, since she was not light of foot unless she chose to be. Ah, but she would not hide it there, where I might discover it. I strained my ears, and her footsteps moved in the direction of her dressing room, which opened off the bedroom: mine was on the opposite side. Now I just had to wait. And wait I did, for several minutes, until I heard wheels and hooves, and realised that Estella must have left by the veranda and driven away.

***

I did not make my move at once; I had been caught out that way before. I recalled the year when I had rushed into the bedroom with great confidence, caught my foot in an innocuous loop of cord lying on the floor, and found myself dangling upside down from the ceiling for a good half hour. I would not be so foolish this time. I looked around me, crept to the bedroom door and inched it open.

Everything was as it should be, but I was far too experienced a campaigner to be taken in. I made a cursory examination of the furnishings, then moved stealthily towards Estella's dressing room. The door stood open, but I advanced crabwise, one step at a time. One cannot be too careful where Estella is concerned.

I entered without incident. As usual, the room was

neat, but I noticed the lowest drawer of the tallboy was not quite shut. That was unlike my wife, who was deliberate in all her undertakings. I opened the wardrobe doors and glanced within, but the lower drawer of the tallboy was on my mind. After perhaps a minute I allowed myself to open the top drawer. Inside were pairs of gloves and fans.

I continued searching, opening each drawer to its fullest extent – about halfway – feeling for contraband, and leaving it precisely as I had found it. Estella must not know I had visited.

My heart thumped as I opened the bottom drawer. Nothing was visible, but if I probed… My fingertip touched an unyielding surface – was it the package? I yelped as something snapped down on my finger. 'Ow!' I cried, and snatched my hand away. On the end of my finger was a mousetrap.

***

I have lost the first round, I thought, as I sat in the bedroom with my hand in a bowl of iced water. But this was merely the first skirmish. The battle was yet to be decided.

With that in mind, I sat back in my chair and pondered. The mousetrap was not my present; one of the rules of the game was that the present must be genuine, and kept in a place where it could be found by the other party. I studied the mousetrap, powerless to harm me since I had disabled the mechanism in my first fit of pique. The trap was of normal size, and while it would have fitted into the package Estella had received, it was not large enough to form the whole. The quest continued. I was sure Estella's sly glance earlier meant that she had something to hide. And by Jove, I was determined to find out what it was.

I consulted my watch and was horrified to see that it was already approaching ten o'clock. I had two hours, perhaps less, to accomplish my goal. Now, Estella had left the bedroom by the veranda and I had not heard her depart. Neither had I heard her footsteps elsewhere in the house, which meant that she could have spent a few minutes in the garden. I rose, padded to the veranda door, and looked outside. The day was beginning to warm up and the servants were emerging one by one to gather petunias and marigolds or pick oranges. My gaze ranged over the scene. She would not have hidden it beneath a bush or in a tree. That was hardly secure, and besides, the sort of clothes Estella wore for meeting with the viceroy did not lend themselves to tree climbing. Neither, for that matter, did Estella, though she was fit, nimble, and strong, as I knew from our weekly self-defence practice sessions. I was about to turn away when I spied the summer house. But of course!

The question now was how to reach the summer house, which stood well back to the left of the garden. I could, as master of the house, saunter into the garden and enter a building whenever I chose – apart from the servants' quarters, which were their domain. However, the servants were sure to tell Avik, who would inform Estella, and she would know I had found her out. And I did not want that. I wanted her to remain in innocence until Christmas Day, or at the very least, to only suspect I had divined her secret, rather than to know that I knew.

I withdrew behind the curtain and considered. The servants were busy on the right-hand side of the garden. If I took great care, perhaps I could sneak past them and gain the summer house. I went to my dressing room and caught up a long black hooded cloak to conceal myself. Then I left the bungalow by the front door, let myself into the garden by the side gate, and crept round the house, keeping in the shadow of trees and shrubs as much as possible. With every minute, I drew closer to my objective. Everyone was busy; no one paid me any heed. I tiptoed to the summer house and tried the door, and to my delight it opened. I slipped in and pulled the door closed.

It was dark inside the summer house, as the windows were small to keep the place cool, and it took my eyes time to adjust. As things grew a little clearer, I was disappointed that the cane chairs and the low table appeared the same as ever. I plumped the cushions, feeling for clues, but nothing was concealed behind or within them. There were no cupboards or hidey-holes, nor any disturbances in the earth floor. I threw the last cushion down with a sigh, then tensed at a sudden creak. I began to turn, but too late. Strong arms pinned me, a foot hooked around my ankle, and I hit the ground like a felled tree, powerless in my adversary's grasp.

A hand yanked off my hood. 'I'm terribly sorry, sir,' said Avik, releasing me and rising. 'I saw someone enter the summer house and thought you were an intruder.' His voice was appropriately sincere, but his eyes held no apology, and I was sure that Estella had set him to watch me.

'Well, I'm not,' I said, getting up with a wince and brushing myself down.

'Your attire confused me,' said Avik.

'Yes, I suppose it would,' I snapped. 'I shall go and change.'

'Sir might also wish to take a bath,' observed Avik, eyeing me, and I had to bite back a retort.

***

Once I had soaked away the shock of my unexpected encounter, and a little of the stiffness that was beginning to set in, as a heavy tackle in one's forties is no laughing matter, I considered my options. My present was not in Estella's dressing room, nor the garden, nor the summer house. She had not concealed it in another room of the house, as far as I knew. In any case, since the bungalow was borrowed and contained only basic furnishings, there were precious few places to hide anything. I knew the parcel's approximate size, but where could it be?

I climbed out of the bath, dried myself and dressed, still pondering, then rang for a cup of mint tea.

It was past eleven; my time was running out. That should have focused my brain, but instead my thoughts chased each other in circles around my head. *Where is that tea?* I growled to myself. Anyone would think Sujit had gone to the Hooghly River for the water, not the kitchen—

The kitchen. I was not familiar with the kitchen, which stood in a separate building near the servants' quarters. In fact, I could not remember ever having entered it. But I was sure it contained lots of places to hide a smallish item.

Now my brain had wings. Once my mint tea had been made and brought, there was no reason for any of the servants to be in the kitchen. A light tiffin would not be served until at least half past one, and more likely two o'clock. Besides, the servants were still busy at their morning tasks, and would not enter a cold building when the sun shone outside.

A knock at the door heralded my mint tea. I thanked Sujit, dismissed him, and almost scalded my mouth on the tea, so eager was I to test my theory. At half past eleven I walked to the veranda, braced myself as if I were a schoolboy in the hundred-yard dash again, and sprinted across the garden.

I heard exclamations as I ran, and murmurings too low for me to understand, but I cared not. I would find that present or die in the attempt.

Sujit was closest to the kitchen, and hurried towards me. 'Sahib, don't go in!'

'I must,' I panted, 'I have to know.' He drew back, trembling, as I flung the kitchen door wide and stepped in.

I barely had time to glimpse the room before a cloud of red powder enveloped me. The top of my head was struck by something which, while not heavy, made a dull thud and blocked my view completely. I put a hand up, and felt cold metal. Then I drew breath and burst into a paroxysm of coughing so violent that I thought I would never get my breath again. Dazed and bewildered, I fell to my knees.

***

The next thing I recall is a hand on mine: a hand in a white cotton glove which looked very familiar.

The metal object was removed from my head. I looked up and saw a bucket, then looked down and saw Estella, who was doing her best not to laugh.

'Papa?'

Surely it couldn't be— Beyond Estella stood Flo and Gus, far taller and more grown-up than I remembered, studying me with puzzled expressions.

'Why are you all red?' Flo asked, her brow

furrowed.

I considered replying, 'Ask your mother.' I also considered replying that I had no idea whatsoever. But in the end, I simply got to my feet and held my arms out. The children rushed towards me, but stopped perhaps a foot away and each extended a hand, which I shook heartily.

'Well, red is the colour of celebration and festivals,' said Estella, with a grin, 'and we do have the children here for Christmas. As for this…' She held her gloved finger to her nose and sniffed. 'I think this is kumkum: turmeric mixed with a bit of lime. The servants must have started preparing for Holi early this year. The festival of colours,' she added, for the benefit of the children. 'Although how a bucket of kumkum came to be on top of the kitchen door…'

'How are the children in Calcutta?' I asked. 'I don't understand.'

'I hope that bucket hasn't caused any permanent damage,' said Estella. Then she grinned. 'When I realised we wouldn't be able to go home for Christmas this year, I wondered whether we could bring the children to India instead. So I wrote to their schools, and both said that provided Flo and Gus kept up with their lessons and had a responsible guardian for the journey, it would be quite all right. Frank Bishop was due to come back out with his wife after his furlough, so I wired, and they were more than happy to do the honours. As for the return journey...' She gave me a speculative look. 'Perhaps we could escort the children ourselves.'

'But how shall we get leave?'

Estella's grin broadened. 'You probably think now that I was fibbing when I said I had business at Government House. However, the viceroy wrote this morning to say that he was prepared to discuss my leave, so I called on him before going to meet the children at the station.' She paused. 'Once I had made arrangements to, um, distract you.'

I blinked. 'So that parcel this morning wasn't important? Or did it have the mousetrap in?'

Estella laughed. 'I'm afraid the parcel wasn't anything to do with it. I saw you watching me open my mail, and thought you might have guessed my little scheme, so I decided to throw suspicion on my poor parcel. Most of its contents are in our bathroom, except for one item which I have here.' She opened her bag and handed me a small wrapped and labelled package. I peered at it: Wright's Coal Tar Soap.

'I think you need it more than I do,' said Estella, and a little giggle escaped from her, like a bubble rising to the top of a still pool.

'Perhaps you're right,' I replied. I dropped the soap, gathered her in an enormous hug, and kissed her full on the lips. 'Or perhaps not,' I added, grinning as our children exchanged exasperated glances.

***

'You're still a bit pink,' said Estella, examining me critically.

'That happens when people throw red powder over one,' I replied, pouring away the scarlet water in the bowl and refilling it. 'I can only presume that you want your husband to resemble a freshly cooked lobster for the next few days.'

'It isn't that bad,' said Estella. 'Anyway, I didn't ask the servants to set up a bucket of kumkum in the kitchen. I merely requested that they keep you occupied for the morning, so that you didn't follow me and spoil the surprise.' She chuckled. 'Although I *will* admit to the mousetrap.'

'The servants certainly managed to keep me busy,' I said, wringing out my sponge. 'You know what's most annoying, though.'

'No, what?' asked Estella, taking the sponge and scrubbing the back of my neck.

'I thought we had done so well to get the children's presents sent in time for Christmas, and now they will be sitting in England with no one to open them.'

Estella smiled. 'I'm sure that Christmas in Calcutta, with elephant rides and exotic food and all sorts of new things to see, will be far more exciting than a tree and presents at home.'

'True,' I admitted. At least Estella's present was arranged. I had bought her a slim gold bangle which would suit her, and not impede her during any of her activities. Perhaps the best thing about my present was that it was waiting at the jeweller's whenever I chose to pick it up. There was no chance of Estella stumbling across it.

I glanced at Estella, who was regarding me thoughtfully. Could she have followed me to the jeweller, and bribed him to tell her what I had chosen? Or had she somehow managed to put the idea of a slim gold bangle into my mind without me realising? But then Estella kissed me, and I decided that whatever the truth was, it was best that I did not know.

***

If you've enjoyed this short glimpse into the world of the Carters, they feature (Mrs Carter in particular) as supporting characters in the *Maisie Frobisher* Victorian mystery series, which begins with *All At Sea*: http://mybook.to/Maisie1. Estella was meant to be a fleeting character, but she ended up being much more important – and I'm tempted to give Estella and Randolph their own spinoff series!

The Case of the Christmas Pudding

'To a medical man, the conclusion should be obvious.'

I jumped, then stared at Holmes, who was regarding me with amusement. 'Whatever do you mean, Holmes?'

'Why, that a walk will do you much more good than a second mince pie.'

'But I never said a word!'

'My dear Watson, gestures and glances may communicate as strongly as words, especially in the case of a man with your speaking countenance.'

I glared at him, discomfited. 'Since we are both meant to be at leisure, Holmes, I did not expect to be observed quite so closely.'

'The period between Christmas and New Year is always slack, but that does not stop my eyes from seeing or my brain from thinking.' Holmes's eyes took on a faraway look. 'I wonder if the criminal fraternity make a point of ceasing their activity for the festive season, and whether that is through choice or necessity. Perhaps there is a monograph in it.' He laughed. 'Oh Watson, do stop fidgeting. This is why you would benefit from a walk.'

'You must admit, Holmes, that it is rather uncomfortable to feel one is being observed like a specimen under a microscope.'

'It was hardly difficult. During the last five minutes you have eyed the crumbs on your plate, gazed at the sky, checked your cup to see how much tea remains in it, then looked back at the plate. I shall not mention the thoughtful hand on the stomach, nor the second glance out of the window. I daresay even Inspector Lestrade would come to the same conclusion.'

I could not help laughing. 'In that case, Holmes, perhaps you should accompany me on this walk. You clearly require stimulation; in fact—'

I was interrupted by a short peal of the doorbell. Holmes raised an eyebrow. 'Perhaps I am wrong about the criminal fraternity.'

Billy's footsteps came upstairs, and the page himself appeared. 'There is a visitor for you, Mr Holmes. A lady.'

Holmes frowned. 'Rather odd that she has not written first.'

'Perhaps she has not had time,' I suggested.

'Perhaps. Does our visitor have a name, Billy? How would you describe her?'

'Her name is Mrs North. She is well dressed, pretty, and no older than twenty-five. Oh, and she says she has come from Hertfordshire.'

'Mmm.'

'Holmes, you have to see her,' I protested. 'It may be really important, especially as she has come into town.'

Holmes sighed. 'My holiday is over. Very well, Watson. Since you are so keen on the idea, we shall see your damsel in distress.' Yet from the way his grey eyes gleamed, I knew he had never intended to turn our visitor away.

***

Our visitor arrived in a flurry of apologies and confusion, and it was all Holmes and I could do to get her to sit. 'Would you like tea, Mrs North?' asked Holmes. 'We have mince pies, too.' This was said with a sly glance at me.

'Tea would be nice,' she replied, 'for it was a trying journey. London is very big, isn't it?'

'Mrs North, please can you tell me why you have come to see me today. This gentleman is my friend Dr Watson, and you may speak before him as confidently as if we were alone.'

Mrs North regarded me with wide china-blue eyes,

and I silently agreed with Billy's assessment of her prettiness. 'A doctor? A medical doctor?'

'I am indeed,' I said, with a smile.

'Then perhaps you can help too. I was in two minds whether to come today, as this is such an odd matter. It seems silly, but I cannot make it out.' She looked perturbed for a moment, and then began her story.

'My name is Dora North, and I live with my husband in Pasden, a village in Hertfordshire. We have been married for six months, and such a thing as this has never happened before. At first I thought nothing of it, but in the days since I have grown more and more worried about him. He has become withdrawn and cold towards me, and I have done nothing to deserve it.' She bit her lip.

'Perhaps if you start from the beginning, Mrs North, that will help us to puzzle this out,' remarked Holmes. To a casual observer he would have appeared calm, but I noted the continual jiggle of his left foot.

'It began on Christmas Day,' said Mrs North. 'We had arranged that my parents, who live nearby, would come to us on Christmas morning. We opened our presents together then, instead of on Christmas Eve, and ate our Christmas dinner. Everything was wonderful, and my husband John was in unusually good spirits; he can be rather quiet sometimes.' She paused, and gazed at Holmes with those wide blue eyes. 'And then Cook brought in the pudding.'

Holmes leaned forward. 'Go on.'

'Once the flames were extinguished, John undertook to serve the pudding. We each had a large helping, as Cook's puddings are uncommonly good. Mamma got the silver wishbone, Papa a silver sixpence, and John got the anchor, but when I cut my piece I found a charm in the shape of a D.' She reached into her bag, brought out a folded handkerchief, and unwrapped it to show a letter D, quite plain and made of silver, with a little loop at the top for a link. Holmes took it, produced a pocket magnifying glass, peered at it for a few seconds, then handed it back.

'I exclaimed in delight and turned to thank John, for I assumed it was a surprise for me. But his face was as white as a sheet, and he stared at my little charm as if it were a poisonous snake.'

'"Is this not from you, dear?" I asked, and with that same strange look he said that it was not.'

'My parents both examined the charm, as surprised as any of us, and said they knew nothing of it. Mamma tried to make the best of it by laughing and saying that it was a little mystery, but John threw down his napkin and got up. When I asked where he was going, he said, "To the kitchen. This must have come from somewhere."'

'"But what about your pudding?" I asked.'

'He looked at me with a mixture of anger and despair such as I have never seen on his face. "I have lost my appetite," he said, and left the room. He did not return, and later a maid brought a message to say that he had gone to bed with a headache. Ever since then he has been very quiet, and I am at a loss to fathom why.'

'I see,' said Holmes.

'That is not the end of it,' she replied, with an expression of mild reproach. 'Yesterday evening, when we were alone, I asked him what he was thinking, as he had not spoken for a whole hour. "I am planning to start a business on the Continent," he said. "You may accompany me or not, as you wish."' Her face twisted in anguish. 'I cannot live abroad; how could I be apart from my parents? And what else can I do? Perhaps he thinks I have done something – something improper, and a man has put the charm in the pudding to woo me, and I don't know what to do!' She burst into noisy tears and buried her face in her hands.

'Please don't worry, Mrs North,' said Holmes, when she had calmed herself a little. 'We shall come back with you on the next train, and see if we can get to the bottom of this matter.'

'That – would be – wonderful,' she choked out. 'I am so terribly afraid. It took all my courage to come here, knowing John might think I had sneaked off to go and meet – *someone*!' This brought on a fresh attack of weeping.

Holmes turned to me. 'Watson, find your Bradshaw; there is no time to lose.'

***

On the train journey to Pasden Mrs North told us a little more of her history. She was her parents' only child, and had lived in the same small village her whole life.

'We were all excited when we heard that the manor house was to let. People speculated on what the new owner would be like, since he was a stranger and quite young, and some said it was a shame that an outsider – one who had been abroad, no less – should take over the manor house. But they soon came round when he made repairs to the roof of the village hall, gave money for a May Day celebration, and organised food parcels for those in need.'

She smiled in reminiscence. 'I was astonished when John spoke to me at a village dance; I never thought anything like that would happen. Not to me, who had lived in the same sleepy village my whole life. How could I be of interest to a man who had seen America and amassed a fortune? But we became acquainted, and by degrees, acquaintance became friendship, then love. How could I not admire such a man?' Her expression changed from awe to distress. 'Now everything is ruined, and I don't know why!'

Holmes put a hand on her arm. 'We shall be at Pasden soon, and then we can begin our investigation. I promise I shall do my best to solve your case.'

'Thank you,' she murmured with tears in her eyes, and I felt a burst of anger against the man who could treat her so cruelly.

The village of Pasden was little more than a picturesque row of shops, a church and a public house, so small that I wondered at it having its own railway station, but the manor house was a Georgian building of mellow stone with large windows and an imposing pillared entrance. Holmes inspected the building. 'Several of the curtains are closed,' he remarked. 'Is part of the house not used?'

'Oh no, all the rooms are in use,' Mrs North replied. 'John sustained an injury to his eyes when he was abroad, and as a consequence he finds bright light difficult to bear.' She touched her right cheek for a moment. 'On a sunny day like today the servants ensure that any room he may use is shielded from direct light.'

'Oh, I see,' said Holmes.

He walked towards the front door, but Mrs North hurried after him. 'Perhaps it would be better if we began at the back of the house.'

Holmes gave her a quizzical look. 'I can certainly talk to the cook, as she is the expert on the pudding. You are right, Mrs North; let us start there.' The relief on her face was unmistakable.

Mrs Latham, the cook, was very willing to talk to us, although it took us some time to get her off the subject of the special recipe for the Christmas pudding which had been handed down from her great-great-grandmother and never failed, not once.

'So when do you make the Christmas pudding?' asked Holmes. 'I assume it is prepared in advance.'

She gave him a pitying glance. 'Only a man would ask that. Why, on Stir-Up Sunday, of course. When else would I do it?' She sighed at my blank expression. 'The last Sunday before Advent, like in the collect: "Stir up, we beseech thee."'

'I see,' said Holmes. 'So, on a Sunday a few weeks before Christmas. Who helps you?'

'Nobody helps me,' Mrs Latham replied indignantly. 'The pudding practically makes itself. The only help I have is when everyone comes into the kitchen to stir the pudding and make a wish.'

'Ah!' cried Holmes. 'Is that when people put the charms in?'

'I put the charms in,' said Mrs Latham firmly. 'I'm not having people putting dirty sixpences in my pudding. I keep the pudding silver packed away specially and I watch everyone while they stir.' She folded her arms.

'So no one could drop an extra charm in the pudding without you noticing?' asked Holmes.

She shook her head. 'Absolutely not.' Her eyes narrowed. 'Why are you so curious about my Christmas pudding, may I ask?'

'I work for a newspaper in London,' said Holmes, 'and our female readers are always interested in recipes and articles on cookery. Word of your pudding came to me, and I wanted to ask for your recipe.'

I doubted Mrs Latham would swallow that, but she preened like a peacock. 'Oh, people often ask me for my recipes.' Then she frowned. 'But it was Christmas three days ago. Why would your readers want a pudding recipe now?'

'We work far in advance,' said Holmes. 'So if you let me have a copy of your recipe, and a list of the charms that you put in it, I'll make sure your name is mentioned.'

While the cook, all smiles, did Holmes's bidding, he glanced at the doors and windows, which were stout and well maintained. 'No signs of a break-in there,' he murmured. 'Mrs North, might I have a word with your husband about the, er, article, if he is at home?'

'He will be at home,' she murmured. 'At this hour he is always in his study.'

She took us to the study door, and Holmes knocked. 'Come!' said a deep voice.

We entered to find the master of the house sitting in an armchair and reading the newspaper. John North was powerfully built, and wore a long bushy beard which would have been more appropriate for an elderly patriarch than a man in his mid-thirties, as I took him to be. As soon as he saw us he rose, and he easily matched Holmes in height. 'Who are you?' he demanded. Even those few words carried a slight but distinguishable American accent.

'My name is Sherlock Holmes, and I am a consulting detective. Your wife visited me earlier today, and I have come to ask you some questions about . . . about one of the charms in your Christmas pudding.'

'I see,' said Mr North. 'Well, I'm afraid that I am busy, and I do not have time to help you. If you wish to know about the pudding, I suggest you speak to the cook.' He sat down and picked up his paper. 'Good day to you.'

We left the room to find Mrs North wringing her hands in the corridor, watched nervously by a young footman. 'You see how he is?' she whispered. 'Normally he is the gentlest, most obliging man.' She gazed at Holmes. 'I am so sorry; you have come all this way for nothing—'

Holmes put his finger to his lips, then beckoned her further along the hall. 'Please do not be distressed, Mrs North. There are people we can speak to besides your husband, and that is what we shall do.' He looked at the closed study door, and his eyes gleamed. 'This case is far from over.'

***

'What else can we do?' asked Dora North, fretfully.

'You mentioned earlier that your parents live nearby,' said Holmes. 'Are they within walking distance, or do we need a carriage?' He eyed the footman, who immediately pretended not to be listening.

'They are but fifteen minutes' walk away. I visit them most days, sometimes twice, and only take the carriage in bad weather.' Her eyes lit up as she spoke, and I saw how she would look when not burdened with fear and worry.

'Then let us set off. I take it they will not mind if you call unannounced?'

'Mind?' She laughed. 'They will be delighted.'

'There, Watson,' Holmes observed, once we had left the manor house and were proceeding towards the village. 'At last you have your walk.'

'Indeed I do,' I replied, slightly out of breath. We had moderated our pace out of consideration for our companion, but if anything she was in danger of outstripping us.

A few minutes later she gestured at a smallish villa on the outskirts of the village. 'Here we are.' She led the way down the path.

The door was opened by an elderly maid who beamed when she saw Mrs North. 'Miss Dora!' Then her smile vanished. 'Who are these gentlemen?'

'Don't worry, Mary, they are just visitors. Are Mamma and Papa at home?'

'They are; I'll go and tell them you're here.'

Mrs North stepped into the hallway and beckoned us forward. 'Come in; they won't mind.'

Holmes and I stepped over the threshold as Mary returned. 'They're taking tea in the – the parlour.' She opened a door on the right and showed us into a room which would have been cramped with half the amount of furniture. Among it all sat a stocky man, perhaps in his fifties, with red cheeks and a bald head, and a slender, pale woman of around the same age who seemed to be composed mostly of frills. Both rose hastily as we came in. On the little table between them was a cake stand half-filled with sandwiches. 'You'll have to introduce the gentlemen, Miss Dora,' the maid said, out of the side of her mouth, 'for I don't know who they are.'

'Mamma, Papa, these gentlemen are Mr Holmes and Dr Watson, and they have come to help me with a puzzle. Gentlemen, these are my parents, Mr and Mrs Sugden.'

'A puzzle, eh?' said Mr Sugden. 'What sort of puzzle would that be?' His expression was neutral, but his tone not particularly welcoming. He glared at his silent wife. 'Invite the gentlemen to a chair, Letitia.'

'Oh – oh yes. Please do sit, gentlemen.'

I looked about me; every chair in the room was covered with antimacassars, fancy work or little cushions, and none appeared comfortable. I lowered myself into the nearest, which was as hard as I had expected, and focused on the couple.

'I had better ask for more cups, hadn't I?' murmured Mrs Sugden.

'Yes, Letitia, you had,' replied her husband, as she rose to pull the bell. 'Not to mention plates.'

'We shall not require plates,' said Holmes, and I must admit to feeling annoyed, since we had missed lunch. 'We only wish to ask you a few questions, then we shall be on our way.'

Mr Sugden frowned. 'What sort of questions? Where are you from? I haven't seen you in the village before.'

'We have come from London,' said Holmes.

'Oh!' breathed Mrs Sugden, gazing at us.

Mr Sugden raised his eyebrows. 'I dare say you have, but why?'

Holmes glanced at Mrs North, who gave him a tiny nod. 'Your daughter is concerned about one of the charms that found its way into the pudding on Christmas Day.'

'Hah!' barked Mr Sugden, and his wife jumped. 'All the way from London, for that?'

'Yes,' said Holmes. 'So it would be very helpful if

you could tell me whether you saw or heard anything unusual at your daughter's house on Christmas Day.' He regarded Mr Sugden with a speculative eye.

'Not a thing,' replied Mr Sugden. 'Well, not until young John took ill and went to bed. Most unlike him; he's as strong as an ox.' He laughed. 'Perhaps it was too much drink taken.' Both his daughter and his wife gave him a pained look.

'Mrs Sugden, did you notice anything unusual on Christmas Day?' Holmes asked.

She gave a nervous giggle. 'Oh no, not at all. I mean, the charm with the letter was a present, wasn't it?'

'Don't be silly, Letitia. John said he had nothing to do with it, and we know we didn't.' Mr Sugden turned to Holmes. 'Any more questions?'

'I'm afraid so. Were you at your daughter's house on the Sunday when the pudding was made? I understand everyone stirs it.'

'Yes, we were, and yes, we did,' replied Mr Sugden. 'We almost always visit Dora for Sunday lunch, and as Cook was making the pudding, naturally we took a turn at stirring.'

'Mrs Latham is an excellent cook,' put in Mrs Sugden.

'That she is,' said Mr Sugden. 'Our Jessie could learn a thing or two from her.'

'I do try,' murmured his wife.

'If it weren't for Sunday lunch at Dora's, I'd have to go to London to get a decent meal,' remarked Mr Sugden, stretching out his legs. 'I go once or twice a month now, to maintain a small interest in my business, and I miss the food most of all.' He glared at his wife. 'Anything else?'

'No, that is all.' Holmes stood up and extended a hand to Mr Sugden. 'Thank you for your time, sir.'

'You can hardly thank us for our hospitality, can you, seeing as Mary never brought those cups. The servants will run wild if you don't keep them in line, Letitia.' Mrs Sugden quailed under his gaze.

The walk back to the manor house was rather less pleasurable than the outward trip. 'Is that your father's usual manner, Mrs North?' asked Holmes.

Dora North considered. 'He's not usually so peppery; I think he was cross that I brought guests without warning.' She paused. 'He is conscious that John is a wealthy man. As a family we were always comfortable, but it is not the same.'

'Yes, he did seem rather short with your mother,' Holmes observed.

A little furrow creased her forehead. 'Papa is not the most patient of men, but he has always been gentle with me.' She met our eyes. 'I do not think my parents' marriage has a bearing on this case,' she murmured. I felt ashamed of myself, though I had not spoken of it.

'My dear Mrs North,' said Holmes, 'at present we do not know *what* has a bearing on the case.'

She sighed. 'You have spoken to Cook and my parents, and John will not help, so I suppose your investigation is at an end.' She looked so utterly helpless that I longed to comfort her.

'Our investigation is not at an end until we have exhausted every avenue,' said Holmes. 'Watson and I shall walk you to the manor house, and then decide our next move.'

She gazed at him. 'I cannot help feeling that it is hopeless.'

We saw Mrs North to the manor house, and with a heavy heart I took the Bradshaw from my pocket.

'Not so fast, Watson.'

I glanced at him. 'What do you mean?'

Holmes did not speak again until we were in the lane. 'Assuming you have no objections, Watson, I would like you to book us accommodation at the local inn for tonight.' He took the Bradshaw from me. 'I shall return to London to pick up a few things, and meet you for dinner.'

'Really? Can you solve the mystery of the Christmas charm, Holmes?'

'The charm is not the mystery,' said Holmes as he strode along. 'Dora North's husband is the mystery.'

***

As promised, Holmes returned by dinner time

carrying a large Gladstone bag. 'I have brought your pyjamas and sponge bag, Watson,' he said, extracting the items and laying them on the bed.

I eyed the bulging bag. 'And…?'

'Wait and see. Now, I propose we have dinner in our room, for reasons which will become apparent.' I raised my eyebrows, but he merely smiled.

Half an hour later, we were both sated. 'Would you like a pint of beer, Watson?' Holmes asked.

'I would,' I replied. 'There are few things more restful than a quiet pint of ale in a country inn, listening to the locals.'

'I agree. Why don't you go down, Watson? I shall join you shortly; I have a small matter to attend to first.'

I was sitting in a quiet corner, nursing the last third of my pint and wondering if Holmes would ever appear, when an elderly, bewhiskered workman shambled in and leaned on the bar. 'Pint of bitter, please, landlord.' When it arrived, he took a large gulp and sighed with satisfaction. 'That hit the spot.' If it had not been for his prominent nose and his height, which he had adopted a stoop to disguise, I would never have recognised in that workman my old friend Sherlock Holmes.

He turned to his neighbour, a dejected-looking young man who seemed somehow familiar. 'Good day, young 'un?'

The young man shrugged. 'I've had better. Came here to take my mind off it.'

Holmes wore a look of concern. 'Why, what's happened?'

'Master gave me a dressing-down,' the man replied. 'Not for doing anything wrong, just for being there.'

'Oh,' said Holmes.

'It ain't like him, that's the funny thing. He's normally easy-going, him and the mistress both. But she brought in a man from London asking questions, and the master wasn't happy.'

'Bit rum,' remarked Holmes. 'Whereabouts do you work? I hope you don't mind me asking, but I'm looking to pick up a bit of trade. I'd rather not go barging in where I'm not wanted, like.'

'Up at the manor house, as a footman. Been there two years, and this is the first time he's raised his voice to me. I didn't answer back – I wouldn't dare – so I went and sat in the kitchen. Cook said my face was turning the cream and if I had nothing better to do I could take an hour off.' A smile flickered over his lips. 'She'd tell you she rules the place with a rod of iron, but she's soft as butter really.'

'Would that be a woman called Mrs Latham?' asked Holmes. 'I've heard of her. Very good cook.'

'She is, and she knows it. Although she's a bit partial to—' The footman tapped his pint glass, which was almost empty.

'Let me get you another of those.' Holmes held up a finger to the barman. 'Partial to what?'

'A little drop now and then.' The footman grinned. 'One of the maids told me she sampled so much of the brandy for the Christmas pudding that she had a little nap at the kitchen table. Someone called for a recipe and had to leave without it because there was no waking her.' He chuckled. 'Good thing it's always high tea on a Sunday evening.'

'Nobody's perfect,' said Holmes. 'If she's a kind soul I might call in and see if she needs any knives sharpening.' He winked at the footman, who smirked and took a long pull at his pint. Presently Holmes finished his own drink, slid the glass across the bar, wished the footman well and ambled out.

It was all I could do not to down my own drink and follow, but I made it last another five minutes before going up to our room. There I found Holmes in his normal clothes and minus whiskers and wig, drying his face. 'Fancy a stroll, Watson?' he asked when he emerged from the towel.

'Where to?' I enquired.

'To the manor house, and you know it. I have a fancy to enquire about a certain visitor on Stir-Up Sunday.'

Ten minutes later we were in the grounds of the manor house and making for the servants' entrance.

Dinner was clearly in progress; Cook was taking a joint of meat from the oven and a maid was draining potatoes. She saw us, banged the colander down, and came to the door. 'What is it?' she snapped.

'We are writing a newspaper article on Mrs Latham's pudding, and we wish to ask a question about the recipe.'

The maid huffed and opened the door wider. 'Recipe, recipe, always a recipe.' She turned. 'Mrs Latham!' she shouted. 'Man here for a recipe.'

Mrs Latham looked over her shoulder. 'Oh, it's you.' She advanced, wiping her hands on her apron. 'Sorry about the noise; it gets busy at dinner time.' She jerked her head towards the scullery, where a skivvy was washing the plates and cutlery from the previous course.

'That's quite all right. May I?' Holmes nodded at the table.

'Of course,' said Mrs Latham, and took a seat herself.

'This is rather an odd question,' said Holmes, 'but I heard at the inn that someone had asked you for one of your recipes on Stir-Up Sunday: a Christmas recipe, I assume. Might we include it in the article?'

Mrs Latham appeared puzzled. 'A recipe? On Stir-Up Sunday?'

The maid who had answered the door to us rolled her eyes. 'They'll be waiting in the dining room, Mrs

Latham. We're already late.'

Holmes turned to the maid. 'I don't suppose you remember? The person I spoke to was quite sure.'

Her eyebrows drew together and she opened her mouth to reply, but at that moment the inner door banged open. John North stood in the doorway, the embodiment of rage. 'What is going on?' He looked at Holmes, seething. 'What are you doing here?'

For once, Holmes had no answer.

'I don't know what you're up to, but if I see you in my house or grounds again, I shall not be answerable for the consequences.' Mr North eyed the servants, who were practically standing to attention. 'Your job is to get dinner on the table at a reasonable time,' he said, in a milder tone, 'not sit chatting with strangers. Do you understand?'

'Yes, sir,' they muttered.

'Good. Now, please get on.' He glared at Holmes and me. 'And you, get out.'

'Well, that's that,' I remarked, as we slunk down the lane with our tails between our legs.

'Perhaps,' said Holmes, 'and perhaps not. I suggest we catch an early train to London in the morning, but we are not beaten yet.' He strode forward, eyes gleaming, like a hound on the scent.

***

When we arrived back in Baker Street, I found myself at a loose end. 'What will you do this morning,

Holmes?'

'I have a couple of errands to run,' Holmes replied. 'Dull, but necessary. What about you, Watson? Will you frowst in a chair again?'

'I shall go for a walk.' The truth was that I could not bear being cooped up in a room. I had spent the train journey fidgeting and worrying about poor Dora – I mean Mrs North – trapped at the manor house with that bear of a man. I glanced at Holmes, hoping he had not somehow read my thoughts, but he merely remarked that the country air seemed to have had a good effect on me, and took his leave.

I spent the walk puzzling over the problem of the pudding, to no avail, and returned two hours later to find Holmes fizzing with nervous energy and holding a telegram. 'This was waiting when I returned a few minutes ago. Look!'

I took the telegram, and read.

Please help STOP John has gone STOP Left goodbye note STOP North.

I gave the telegram back to Holmes. 'Perhaps it is for the best. They are not well suited at all. She is so delicate, and he is so—'

'Physical appearance is not everything, Watson,' Holmes chided. 'Handsome is as handsome does.'

I snorted. 'It is not like you to quote old saws,

Holmes.'

'Never mind that.' Holmes dashed to the bureau and picked up a scrawled note. 'I shall take this down for Billy to wire, and then we must be off.'

I stared at him. 'What, to the manor house?'

'Watson, there is no time for that!' Holmes ran downstairs as if John North himself were chasing him, and I had no choice but to follow.

***

Two minutes later we were in a cab. 'This is our best chance,' said Holmes. 'When a man like John North says he is leaving, he goes far. I just hope we arrive in time.'

'Are we going to the docks?' I asked.

'What? No, Watson, to Euston station. John North has the advantage of us, but we can still catch him if we get through this traffic.' He glared at the busy street.

'What did you put in the wire?' I asked.

'I asked Mrs North to come to London directly and wait at Baker Street until we return.' Holmes looked out of the window and fidgeted. 'Come on, come on,' he muttered.

At last we arrived at the station. Holmes flung half a sovereign to the cabbie, then dashed towards a porter leaning against a pillar. 'Has the Liverpool express gone yet?' he demanded.

The porter, completely unruffled, pointed at a

distant, crowded platform where a train squatted. 'You'll be wanting that one. It goes in a quarter of an hour.'

'Thank you,' said Holmes, and we ran along, dodging porters and passengers and suitcases, until we arrived at the correct platform.

A station official stood facing the train, hands clasped behind his back. 'Is this the Liverpool express?' Holmes asked.

He inspected us from under his cap. 'It is, gentlemen, but you may not board. The train is not yet ready.' He eyed the gathered passengers, who sagged at his pronouncement.

'Watson, can you check the platform for Mr North.' Holmes turned to the official. 'We do not wish to board; I merely have a message for a former colleague of mine. I believe he intends to travel on this train.'

The official raised his eyebrows. 'He had better hurry, for we depart at noon.'

I dashed up and down the long platform, but in vain; John North was not there. Then the official shouted, 'Passengers, you may board.' A frantic scramble ensued, and I was almost propelled onto the train by the rush of passengers.

Eventually I arrived at Holmes's side. 'Any luck?' I panted.

Holmes shook his head, and we both glanced at the

station clock, which showed six minutes to twelve. We watched the approach to the platform for the tall, broad form of John North, but there was no sign of him.

'If you would move back, please, gentlemen,' said the official.

Holmes looked crestfallen, and my heart went out to him. He had been so confident, and it had come to nothing. 'Perhaps he is planning to take a later train,' I said.

'I was so sure,' murmured Holmes.

The official stepped forward and raised his whistle.

Holmes eyed him. 'Perhaps we could wire the station in Liverpool—'

He stiffened as a tall figure ran towards us, and a loud voice shouted 'Wait!'

As the figure came closer I recognised John North. He was sprinting for the train, somewhat hampered by a large new carpet bag and a voluminous ulster. He wore a deerstalker, with the ear flaps tied under his chin.

Holmes moved forward to bar his way. 'No, Mr North, *you* wait.'

John North glared at him. 'Stand aside, sir.'

Holmes stood firm. 'No, I shall not. I know your secret – I know the truth – and I urge you to stay for your wife's sake.'

Mr North stood, breathing heavily, and suddenly

he seemed smaller than before. 'You know?'

'I do,' said Holmes. 'There is no need for you to run away, Mr North. Please return with me, and we shall resolve this once and for all.'

The official eyed us, his whistle at his lips. 'Are you boarding this train, sir, or not?'

Still looking at Holmes, John North shook his head, and the whistle shrilled. The train huffed in response, and as it began to glide out of the station Mr North followed us from the platform like a sleepwalker. Holmes hailed a cab, and seconds later we were bound for Baker Street once more.

***

'Is this really necessary, Holmes?' I asked, as we waited in the manor-house kitchen, doing our best to keep out of the way of the bustling servants.

'I have my methods, Watson.'

'I don't mind,' said John North. 'Now that Dora knows, I don't mind anything.' His smile erased the severity from his face and made him look years younger.

A maid came into the kitchen. 'They're ready for the starter, Mrs Latham.'

'In that case,' said Holmes, 'our time has come.' He led the way to the dining room then stood aside for John North, who took a deep breath, drew himself up, and entered. Mrs North beamed at him, but her parents, sitting on either side of her, gaped as if he had risen from the dead.

Dora North rose from her seat at the head of the table and gestured to her husband to take it, but he waved Holmes forward. 'I fancy this gentleman will be doing most of the talking. I shall go to the kitchen and ask for three more places to be laid.'

A few minutes later, everyone was settled at table. 'I shall begin, as I do not wish to delay your meal for longer than necessary,' said Holmes. 'This has been a most curious case; what seemed a Christmas novelty became perhaps one of the strangest matters I have ever dealt with.'

'Mrs North called me in to investigate the mysterious appearance of a silver charm in her Christmas pudding. The charm was in the shape of a letter D, and understandably she assumed it was meant for her. When her husband reacted angrily, her only explanation was that since no one at the table had put the charm in the pudding, he might suspect her of dalliance with another. I dismissed this idea at once – what suitor would reveal his hand so publicly? Moreover, Mr North's instantaneous reaction to the D made it clear that the charm was intended for him. What could be so frightening about the letter D?'

Holmes poured himself a glass of water from the carafe on the table, took a sip, then continued. 'My first line of enquiry was to investigate how the charm had got into the pudding. To that end I spoke to Mrs

Latham and found that the pudding was made on Stir-Up Sunday, a few weeks before Christmas. Everyone in the house had stirred the pudding, but she had watched throughout. This seemed watertight, unless someone was in league with the cook and had slipped the charm in with her knowledge. However, given Mrs Latham's obvious pride in her work, this was unlikely. Mr North declined to speak to me on that occasion—'

'Sorry,' murmured John North.

Holmes smiled at him, then addressed the table in general. 'My next move was to speak to Mrs North's parents, Mr and Mrs Sugden, who were in the manor house both at Christmas dinner and during the making of the pudding, and see whether they had any information for me. They provided no fresh insights on the pudding or the charm, and therefore I decided to exploit local knowledge and repair to the village inn. There I learnt that an individual had called at the manor house on Stir-Up Sunday, found the cook taking a well-deserved nap, and, after waiting for some time, left again. I could hardly ask my interlocutor who that person was, so I determined to enquire at the manor-house kitchen, whereupon Mr North threw me out.'

'I am truly sorry,' muttered John North, now distinctly pink beneath his beard.

'Oh no, it was extremely helpful. It gave me the opportunity to note that, though you were in a brightly lit kitchen and you allegedly had weak eyes, you did not shield them from the light.'

Mr and Mrs Sugden gave him a surprised look, but said nothing.

'Dr Watson and I returned to London the next morning. I told Watson I was running errands, but in reality I was continuing with the case. When I examined the charm, I saw a maker's mark: the letters *IG* beneath a crown. That denoted a famous jeweller's: Garrard in Regent Street. After making enquiries there, I discovered a special order had been placed several weeks earlier for a bespoke silver charm in the shape of a D. The order was paid for that day and eventually posted to an address in Hertfordshire.'

Holmes gazed around the table. 'Why would the person who ordered the charm choose such a way to deliver their message? Why wouldn't they speak to Mr North? My conclusion was that they were not confident in their knowledge, or too intimidated to challenge him. Far easier to put the charm in the pudding and await a result. If they were wrong, Mr North would not react, his wife would assume the charm was for her, and no harm would be done. If he did react – and he did – there must be a foundation for our mystery person's suspicions.'

'This is ridiculous!' Mr Sugden huffed with disdain. 'Who would do things in such a roundabout, underhanded way?'

Slowly, Mrs Sugden stood up. 'I did it,' she said, and her voice was steady, though she shook like a leaf.

***

'*What?*' Mr Sugden shouted. 'What do you mean, Letitia?'

'I saw it, and I had to do something.'

'You saw what?' demanded her husband. 'Of all the stupid things—'

'She was trying to protect her daughter,' said Holmes.

'I couldn't tell what it meant,' said Mrs Sugden, her voice a little stronger, 'but I knew it was bad. I formed a plan, and went to London to do some early Christmas shopping. I had hoped to put the charm in the pudding when I stirred it, but Cook was watching, so I returned later that afternoon when I thought she might be asleep or, um, distracted. The pudding bowl was on the table with a cloth over it, so I slipped the charm in.' She covered her mouth with her hands and gazed at her daughter with wide eyes that, though faded by time, would once have been the same shade of blue as Mrs North's. 'You don't know how worried I was—'

'What did you see, Letitia?' bellowed her husband.

John North rose from his seat and turned the lights up. 'She saw this.' He presented his right cheek to us, moving the hair of his beard this way and that, and bit by bit revealed a pale, raised scar which formed a large D. 'The beard hides it well, but the hair has never grown where I was branded.'

'What!' shouted Mr Sugden, his eyes almost popping out of his head. 'What are you, a common felon?'

'When I was a boy, I lived in a Whitechapel slum with my mother. As often happens, I fell in with the local gang: the Dorset Street Lads. I was big for my age, and they said I would be useful. At first I was just a lookout, but after a year the older lads judged it was time I earned my keep. They wanted me to turn pickpocket, but I refused, and I could defend myself. I had to get out, but I didn't know how.'

He paused, and swallowed. 'One day I was keeping watch as usual and along came a policeman. I whistled, and the lad I was looking out for came pelting round the corner, gave me a bundle of handkerchiefs, and fled. I was so surprised that I was caught red-handed. It was my first offence, but because of my size they thought I must be older than I was and made an example of me. I was whipped and sent to the reformatory school for two months.' He winced. 'I shall not say what happened there, but I knew I would never go back.'

Mrs North gave him her hand, and he enclosed it in his own large one. 'As soon as I got out I went to the gang leaders and told them I was leaving, but they said no one ever left the gang. When I tried to run they caught me, tied me up, then heated an iron and branded me on the cheek. D for Dorset Street and D for deserter.' He touched his face self-consciously.

A tear ran down Dora North's cheek in sympathy. 'I thought your scar was from the injury that hurt your eyes, dearest.'

John North hung his head, and resumed his narrative with difficulty.

'I had to leave, both for my safety and my peace of mind, so I slipped onto a train bound for Liverpool. I had seen the White Star Line posters on my occasional trips outside the slum – I could read well enough to pick out the word *America* – and the gang would never follow me there.'

'I managed to stow away for half the voyage, and luckily when the crew found me they were lenient. They put me to work in the kitchen and gave me a straw mattress to sleep on, and at the end of the voyage they even gave me a few dollars to get started. I began as a boot boy in a New York hotel, and as soon as I could hide my disfigurement with a beard I sought new opportunities. To summarise, fifteen years later I had several people working for me in a thriving business, and I had made more money through investments.'

He sighed. 'But I missed home. So when I was

fairly sure that I could live independently if I never did another day's work in my life, I sold up and came back to England. It had been twenty years since I left and I was confident no one would recognise me, having discovered on my return that my mother had died. To make sure, I took up residence in a quiet village.'

Holmes nodded. 'Having noticed your curious scar in the kitchen, I recognised it as a gang mark which suggested you had had dealings with the Dorset Street Lads. After visiting the jeweller this morning, I proceeded to the newspaper archives and spent a fruitful hour searching for news of gang members sentenced to imprisonment between fifteen and twenty-five years ago.' He smiled. 'I looked for young lads, since I thought it unlikely anyone would have been able to brand you once you reached your full size.' Holmes reached into the inner pocket of his jacket and passed Mr North a scrap of paper. 'I believe this refers to you.'

John North read the paper. 'Yes, that was me. "Jack South, twelve, convicted of petty larceny and sentenced to a whipping and two months' imprisonment."' He grimaced. 'It was a terrible experience, but it probably saved me from the gallows.'

'You turned your whole life upside down,' said Holmes. 'You changed your name from Jack South to

John North, and arrived in America a different man.'

'I am so sorry.' Mrs Sugden's voice trembled. 'If I had known… I do hope that one day you can forgive me.'

'Forgive him?' shouted Mr Sugden. 'He is a common criminal, and married to our daughter! His name isn't even his own – you heard him!' He stood up. 'Dora, you had better come with us; who knows what this man might do.'

'No!' cried Mrs North, moving to her husband's side. 'John is no criminal. He is my husband, and I love him.'

Mr Sutton glared at her. 'If you are determined to throw your lot in with this man…' He transferred the glare to his wife. 'Letitia, we are leaving. When that man began his story I assumed this was another of your idiotic fancies, but it appears that for once you are right.'

'I was wrong,' said Mrs Sugden, 'and my son-in-law's story has made me realise my mistake. When I saw the mark on Mr North's cheek, I thought he was a murderer or worse. I was terrified Dora might be in danger; but I also feared she had married a man whom she would grow to hate.'

She gave her husband a look that spoke volumes. 'You have always been forthright, but you never used to bully and shout at me: not until Dora left our home. It is time for you to mend your ways, Ernest, and treat me as your wife, not an object of ridicule and a scapegoat.' She turned to John North. 'Once again, I am truly sorry, and I hope you can forgive me.'

Mr North came round the table and took her hand. 'I wish you had come to me first; then I would have told you the story. Apart from that, there is nothing to forgive.'

Mrs Sugden began to weep, and John North put a large, hesitant arm around her shaking shoulders. Dora North rushed to her mother, while Mr Sugden put his hands in his pockets, walked to the window, and stared into the night.

Holmes caught my eye, and we slipped away. 'Our part in this affair is concluded,' he murmured. 'If we hurry, we can catch the last train to London. But first I shall tell the kitchen to send the starter in. Perhaps food will smooth things over.'

***

I gazed out of the window as the train rattled along.

'A penny for your thoughts, Watson. We are ten minutes from Euston station, and you have barely said a word the whole way home.'

'It was so very unexpected,' I replied. 'I honestly thought Mr North would be the villain.'

'Under that beard and that imposing stature, he is a good and soft-hearted man. You saw how he was with the servants.'

'Yes.' I sighed. 'But it seems unfair that you have given the Norths such a generous Christmas present while we leave empty-handed.'

'Quite the contrary. Do you remember when John North came into the kitchen and returned the slip of paper I had given him? Folded inside was a cheque which more than repays the time and trouble we have spent on this case.'

'Oh.' I returned my gaze to the window.

The snap of Holmes's watch case made me turn round. 'Five more minutes,' he said. 'Since we have barely eaten with all the excitement, I propose we repair to the Strand on arrival and treat ourselves to a slap-up dinner at Simpson's, on the promise of Mr North's handsome cheque.'

I managed a smile, though I did not much feel like it; perhaps hunger was making me low-spirited. 'What a good idea, Holmes.' Then I paused, remembering a pair of imploring china-blue eyes. 'I shall forego dessert, though. I shall not be able to look a pudding in the face for a very long time.'

**

If you've enjoyed this fairly traditional Sherlock Holmes tale, you might also like my *Halloween Sherlock* series of Holmes novelettes (and the omnibus includes an exclusive short story); http://

mybook.to/HSherlock.

If you prefer your Sherlock with a twist, my *Mrs Hudson & Sherlock Holmes* series narrates some early adventures through the eyes of Mrs Hudson, beginning with *A House of Mirrors*: http://mybook.to/Mirrors.

Alternatively, you can meet Holmes and Watson in the company of Jack Hargreaves, a young woman who has been ducking and diving ever since she ran away from her past. Her story begins with *A Jar of Thursday*: http://mybook.to/jrtsdy.

About the Author

Liz Hedgecock grew up in London, England, did an English degree, and then took forever to start writing. Eventually, some short stories crept into the world. A few even won prizes. Then the stories began to grow longer…

Now Liz travels between the nineteenth and twenty-first centuries, murdering people. To be fair, she does usually clean up after herself.

Liz's reimaginings of Sherlock Holmes, the Caster & Fleet Victorian mystery series (written with Paula Harmon), the Maisie Frobisher Mysteries, the Magical Bookshop series and the Pippa Parker cozy mystery series are available in ebook and paperback.

Liz lives in Cheshire with her husband and two sons, and when she's not writing or child wrangling you can usually find her reading, messing about on Twitter, or exploring museums and art galleries. That's her story, anyway, and she's sticking to it.

Website/blog: http://lizhedgecock.wordpress.com
Facebook: http://www.facebook.com/lizhedgecockwrites
Twitter: http://twitter.com/lizhedgecock
Goodreads: https://www.goodreads.com/lizhedgecock
Amazon author page: http://author.to/LizH

Cover Credits

Tree and presents image (background recoloured): Flat design Christmas tree free vector by pikisuperstar at freepik.com (https://www.freepik.com/free-vector/flat-design-christmas-tree_10893969.htm).

Cover and headings font: Roller Coaster by Design and Co (https://thehungryjpeg.com/store/design-and-co).

Cover made using GIMP image editor: https://www.gimp.org.

Books by Liz Hedgecock

To check out any of my books, please visit my Amazon author page at http://author.to/LizH, or search for 'Liz Hedgecock' on Amazon. If you follow me, you'll be notified when I release a new book.

Maisie Frobisher Mysteries (4 novels)
When Maisie Frobisher, a bored young Victorian socialite, goes travelling in search of adventure, she finds more than she could ever have dreamt of. Mystery, intrigue and a touch of romance.

Caster & Fleet Mysteries (6 novels, with Paula Harmon)
There's a new detective duo in Victorian London . . . and they're women! Meet Katherine and Connie, two young women who become partners in crime. Solving it, that is!

Pippa Parker Mysteries (6 novels)
Meet Pippa Parker: mum, amateur sleuth, and resident of a quaint English village called Much Gadding. And then the murders began…

The Magical Bookshop (4 novels)
An eccentric owner, a hostile cat, and a bookshop with a mind of its own. Can Jemma turn around the second-worst secondhand bookshop in London? And can she learn its secrets?

Mrs Hudson & Sherlock Holmes (3 novels)
Mrs Hudson is Sherlock Holmes's elderly landlady. Or is she? Find out her real story here.

Sherlock & Jack (3 novellas)
Jack has been ducking and diving all her life. But when she meets the great detective Sherlock Holmes, they form an unlikely partnership. And Jack discovers that she is more important than she ever realised…

Halloween Sherlock (3 novelettes)
Short dark tales of Sherlock Holmes and Dr Watson, perfect for a grim winter's night.

For children (with Zoe Harmon)
A Christmas Carrot

Printed in Great Britain
by Amazon